MW00743702

Copyright © 2002 by Phil Martin.

Library of Congress Number:		2002095684
ISBN :	Hardcover	1-4010-8140-1
	Softcover	1-4010-8139-8

This book was printed in the United States of America.

To order additional copies of this book, contact:
Xlibris Corporation
1-888-795-4274
www.Xlibris.com
Orders@Xlibris.com
16616

THE LONG
JOURNEY
HOME

To Gary,
I hope you Enjoy
this!

BONNA FORTUNA!

Phil mata

Jackie Rossiter, age 8, March 1943

THE LONG JOURNEY HOME

Phil Martin

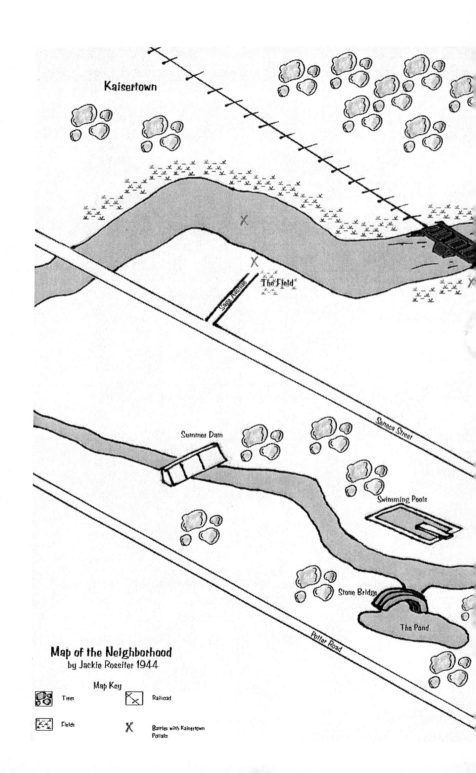

Kaisertown

The Field

Saga Avenue

Seneca Street

Summer Dam

Swimming Pools

Stone Bridge

The Pond

Potter Road

Map of the Neighborhood
by Jackie Rossiter 1944

Map Key

Trees   Railroad

Fields   X   Battles with Kaisertown Potato

For those who give meaning to my life
Geri, Karen, Lisa and Kristin

In memory of Bill and Clara, Patsy, Billy, Joan and Mary

CONTENTS

THE LONG JOURNEY HOME
By Phil Martin

It's retirement time—a time of life when perception clashes with reality
Perception is when the house you've lived in for so many years seems larger
Now that the kids are gone
Reality comes with the death of a friend—whose age was the same as yours

During walks in the neighborhood you begin to notice
That your new neighbors are about the same age as your children
You're in a time warp . . . you feel lost in the future
It's then that you realize the many years it's been since your own parents passed away

Perspective distorts time: A month seems like a week—a year seems like a few months
At weddings and wakes you see old friends not seen for thirty years or more
You're glad to see them—you begin to reminisce
And that's when you're reminded of how many years . . . so many years

The stress of the job is gone now; the blood pressure is thankfully down, and you
Wonder to yourself: So why am I getting to know the doctor and pharmacist so well?

You secretly curse the assembly line in the doctor's office—you long for the days
When "Doc" was a neighbor—who lived just down the street

Are these new ailments—or was I just too busy to notice?
Why do I have all these aches and pains now?
I guess I was just too busy to notice

Sometimes a ghost of the distant past will streak through your mind in a flash
Then just as quickly be gone
When it's over you find that the flash has delivered you back to the past
Back to the days of your boyhood—to the 'forties and 'fifties again

Before you know it you find yourself driving around that old neighborhood where you
Grew up, looking for something that's no longer there . . . The people are all gone now
And all that's left are the old houses . . . and memories of a time that has passed

You squint through the window of the empty classroom to see if it still looks the same
As you see your own reflection in the glass—you realize that the guy staring back . . .
Is the one you've been searching for
You've found the time and place that used to be . . .
You've found the boy that once was me

"As our life passes so quickly through the years and decades into our "senior years," the sharp contrast of the present compared to the days of our youth becomes increasingly visible. When we're nearing the end of a long journey, it's only natural to want to look back to see how far we've come and what it was like when we first started out. Some of the finest memories that we have in later life are from those days of our youth—when our world was full of the excitement of discovery and the wonder of so many new experiences. Those memories from our youth help to keep us young—all the way to the end of our journey."

—Jackie Rossiter, age 67, circa 2002

"There's only two kinds of people in this world: Irish, and those who wish they were Irish!"

—"Fisty" Mullaney, age 12, circa 1944"

"Grandpa, what was it like when you were a boy during the war? I bet it was really different back then, huh?"

When I sold the family business and retired, my ten-year-old grandson was always asking what it was like when I was a boy growing up in the nineteen forties during World War Two. I answered a few of Jackie's questions, but the more I told him about those days the more he wanted to know. And then, because of Jackie's questions, I began to remember things that I thought I had forgotten a long time ago. My newly awakened memories began to draw me slowly back in time to those fun days when I was a boy. I have to admit that I wanted to tell the story as much as Jackie wanted to hear it.

"But Jackie, before I go all the way back to the beginning of the story I have to tell you about these two young men driving an old car across France in October of 1956."

-CHAPTER ONE-

A PROMISE TO KEEP

The motor in the old Simca was groaning as they headed west across the French countryside towards the coast. The early October fall colors on the trees and the rolling hills and vineyards of France reminded the two young American airmen of the place where they had grown up. They arrived at their base in eastern France just three months earlier, so it was reassuring to see that the landscape looked so familiar. They were in their early twenties and had never been so far away from home, but they would never admit to being homesick. When they were young boys they had learned to hide their fears—especially when around other people.

Their knowledge of the French language would improve over the next thirty-three months, but at this point they could only speak and understand a few basic expressions. In spite of their fears and inexperience, they knew that this trip would be their first priority. For them it was a sacred pledge. Shortly after arriving in France they pooled their money together to buy the old car so they could make this journey. It was as if they were on a mission; there would be no other travel until this promise was taken care of. They had joined the Air Force together, and after technical schools were assigned to the medical corps. It was only through a coincidence that they were both ordered to the same duty station at the same time. They were convinced that fate had brought them together in France so they could make this journey together. As the old car rattled on, they were both lost in their thoughts about their boyhood. They spoke only a few words during the nine-hour drive.

"I wish he could be here with us today."

"Yeah, I wish they could all be here."

"Who knows, maybe they are."

"You know, you might be right."

They drove on in silence towards their long-anticipated destination.

-CHAPTER TWO-

LOOKING BACK THROUGH

THE REAR VIEW MIRROR

"Jackie, you know my strongest memory of World War Two was the sound of church bells."

"Church bells?"

"Yep, that's right, I'll never forget that day in May of nineteen forty-five when we heard about the surrender of Germany, finally ending three and a half years of war for us in Europe. For many years afterwards, we called that day 'VE Day.' At the time, I was just a few months past my tenth birthday. I can even recall that it was a nice spring day. Me and my best friends, 'DJ' Corrigan, 'Fisty' Mullaney and Jimmy Finnegan went running down to the corner of Seneca Street to see what all the commotion was about. Well, what we saw were all these busses, cars and trucks stopped right in the middle of the street. Horns were blowing and hundreds of people were dancing around in the street. Everyone was hugging and kissing because we had just won the war. The end of the war meant that our fathers, uncles, brothers, cousins and friends would soon be coming home, and we wouldn't have any more fear of war. And you know what? The word 'peace' had a deep and powerful meaning for us that day. And then the bells at Saint Bridget's Church suddenly started ringing, and they kept on ringing until late at night—long after the celebration in the street was over. Well, I don't know why, but the sound of those bells has stayed in my memory ever since that day. Yeah, I'll never forget that day.

"You see Jackie, back then life was fun and uncomplicated

when I was a boy growing up in that Irish neighborhood. We all lived in a very innocent time in our own little ethnic neighborhoods. In our neighborhood, we were all poor, all Catholic and all Irish. Well, maybe not everyone, but for the most part anyway. Over the years, the religion and the Irish backgrounds have blurred some in my memory, but the memory of the poverty—well, that's something that you never forget, son. And Jackie, since those days we've lost something so very valuable: a sense of belonging. During those times each one of us felt that we were part of a fraternal group. We had an *identity.*

"Say, Jackie, I've been meanin' to take a ride out to my old neighborhood to see what it looks like now. Would you like to come along with me?"

"I sure would, Grandpa."

Well, Jackie and I drove all around South Buffalo together. I showed him the places that meant so much to me in those days. I hadn't been back there in a long time, so I was curious myself about how everything looked. I showed him the soda fountain where I worked as a fourteen-year-old, and the Catholic Church where I served Mass as a ten-year-old. Then I took him to my special place, Cazenovia Park. That's the place where I had spent so many hours fishin', swimmin' and just havin' a real good time with my buddies, Fisty, DJ and Jimmy.

We visited the old neighborhood several times, and eventually I took him to my all-time favorite spot: "The Old Log" on Cazenovia Creek. "Jackie, this is the place that holds so many good memories for me that I don't even know where to start. Well, let's see, I guess I should start with the beginning of the war, December seven, nineteen forty-one. I was almost seven years old, and that date will stand out in my mind forever. You see, that's because we were so young that the war had all of us kids really scared. I remember how I thought that the Nazis and the Japanese were lurking in the shadows in my bedroom at two o'clock in the morning. I used to wake up in a sweat, and I had nightmares of them cutting my throat because at that age my imagination always had me believing the worst. We had something called air-raid drills during the night. Loud, shrieking sirens would wake everyone, and then a warden would come around to the houses in the dark and yell outside your window, 'Turn those lights off! Turn that radio off! Do you want the enemy to know where to drop the bombs?' I didn't realize that they were only practice drills, so my nightmares were really bad after the air raids."

Jackie was really interested in hearing about those days so we decided to come back to "The Old Log" every time we got a chance. Sometimes we brought a couple of fishing lines to drop in the water while we talked. Back then I had a good memory, so I told him the whole story about the war, his great grandfather and great grandmother, and all of the other people who were still there in my memory after so many years. I could actually still see all of them as clearly as if it was yesterday. In my imagination it was nineteen forty-one, and I was a seven-year-old boy all over again. Every time we came back to "The Old Log," we talked for hours and hours.

This is a story about all of those good people of the nineteen forties and World War Two. Although it's about the people of an Irish-American neighborhood, it could just as well have been a story about any other ethnic city neighborhood during those years of war when the problems were the same for the families all over the country. It's a story about those good people "on the home front," the adults who sent their teenagers off to war somewhere on the other side of the world for three and a half years. During those days one of the worst problems was the anxiety that came because of what we didn't know. Information about your relatives fighting in the war was very slow in coming. Back then the world was a much bigger place for all of us. It was a time before rapid communications and high-speed airplane travel. Mysterious sounding places with war-time names like Iwo Jima and Anzio seemed so far away from Buffalo, New York. The world was *so big* then.

The adults had suffered through a bad depression in the nineteen thirties, and some of the men had even fought in the

First World War. Now they were suffering the loss of their children, fathers, uncles and brothers—either killed, wounded or were missing in action. In spite of their daily hardships they found the time for us young people. They protected us and gave us a sense of security while the war was going on all over the world. These were the people who held our country together while their own children went off to fight in the war.

"You know, Jackie, myself and all the other young kids from back in those days will always be thankful to the young men who went off to fight in that war. But, we'll also be thankful to the adults who stayed behind to watch over us kids. You see, we were all really afraid during the war so we needed reassurance from the adults who stayed home—and we got that reassurance and protection from all of them.

"Our neighborhood was made up mostly of immigrants from Ireland, as well as the sons and daughters of immigrants. My parents came from Canada and Newfoundland, but their parents were from Ireland. My dad drove a bus on the Seneca Street route, and when he was working, he watched out as he drove by to see if we were out after dark. The rule was that you had to be in the house as soon as the streetlights came on during school days. If you weren't home when the streetlights came on, you were in big trouble. My dad came to this country from an orphanage in Ontario, Canada after his parents passed away. Believe it or not, he was actually smuggled across the border in the bottom of a hay wagon by his uncle Joe."

"A hay wagon! Why would he do that, Grandpa?"

"Well, that's hard for us to understand now Jackie, but in those days people didn't have much education, and they didn't trust the government at all. They were afraid of the government because the government in the old country many years before had mistreated them. They always called Ireland the 'old country.' Since my dad didn't have his citizenship he worried about being arrested every time we crossed the border to visit my mother's sisters in

Toronto. One day some of Dad's friends told him it would be easier to get your citizenship if you volunteered to join the military. Now if anything scared my mom it was the thought of Dad going off to war and leaving her alone with five young kids. Three of Dad's nephews had already joined the military service during that year, so Mom was really afraid that somebody was going to be killed. When she was upset she would always use the name of The Holy Family as a form of prayer.

"'Jesus, Mary and Joseph, Mike—now don't be talkin' like that, will ya'! Let's just be thankful that Mikey and Jackie are too young ta go!' Mikey was my older brother—he was twelve years old. And I had three sisters: Margaret, Maureen and Mary. Maureen and Margaret were older than me, and Mary was the youngest.

"It seemed that just about everybody in the neighborhood was Catholic, so most people didn't ask what street you lived on, but they did ask, 'What's your parish?' Our parish was Saint Bridget's, and our street was Sage Avenue. Memories of Sage Avenue have stayed in my mind more than any other street that we lived on. To this day it's that extra special place in all of my memories because my cousins, the Rossiter and the McDonald families also lived on Sage. Because of them I felt safe and protected from the scary world the war brought to us from the outside. The three families all lived on the same side of the street, nearly equal numbers apart. I don't know why, but all my life I thought that was some sort of a 'fate' thing. I remember my uncle Jim McDonald was always painting his house. Those old houses were built real narrow and very high on tiny lots. There were usually three floors, including a third-floor attic where old things were stored. Sometimes the attic was used as an extra bedroom for the boys in the family. It was easy for us kids to imagine any of those tall, narrow houses as a haunted house so we made up plenty of ghost stories about one of the real spooky-looking houses on the street. If you didn't own the house you lived in, it was usually called a 'double' house, with two families living in the house, one upstairs, and one downstairs. My cousins owned their homes at number nineteen and number fifty-one, while we rented a lower unit at number eighty-one.

"You know, Jackie, the war dominated almost every part of our daily life. It seemed that almost every family had a son or daughter serving in some branch of the military by the time the war ended in nineteen forty-five. On the radio there was news everyday about the war, and on the weekend when we went to the movies, the news about the war filled up most of the newsreel programs. At church on Sundays the priest was always reminding us to say prayers for all of the boys fighting in the war, and many times we were asked to pray for the family of a soldier who had been killed or captured by the enemy. The adults talked about the war every time they got together, and we would always hear them asking about the son or father of one of their friends or relatives who were serving in the military. There were so many boys killed or wounded that we always knew the families that were affected. By the time the war ended in nineteen forty-five, there were over twelve million people serving in the military. Because the population of the country back then was less than half as much as it is today, that would be like having over twenty-five million people serving in the military now! Huge supplies of just about everything were needed to fight such a massive war, so the government had to ration many items that were in short supply. Rationing was necessary because the massive military buildup had to have priority on any item that would be in short supply. There were many everyday items that we couldn't purchase or were rationed by the government. Automobiles, bicycles, fuel oil, gasoline, kerosene, shoes, stoves, tires and many foods were rationed. To be able to buy certain kinds of food, every family was issued a book of ration coupons that had to be presented at the store when making a purchase. Coupon tickets were needed to buy such things as sugar, butter and coffee. All of the cars had letters on the windshield that indicated just how much gasoline could be purchased each month. The amount of gasoline a person was allowed to have would be determined by the importance of their job to the 'National Defense,' or the good of the country.

"My mom, now that would be your great-grandmother, used to complain that she couldn't buy nylon stockings because all of the nylon was being used to make parachutes for the military. In fact, there were so many shortages that the government asked everybody to help collect some of the scrap materials that were necessary to fight the war. All during the war there was a truck trailer parked on a vacant lot next to the McDonald house near the corner of Seneca Street. All of us kids went around the neighborhood collecting newspapers, rags, copper wire, and tin foil from the inside of cigarette packs, and then we took those things to the big trailer. We were told that what we were doing was for the 'war effort'—a phrase we heard many times during the war. We were also told that we were being very patriotic—also a phrase we would hear many times during the war. I figured that collecting scrap was a good way for me to get even with those throat-cutting Nazis and 'dirty little Japs' for coming into my bedroom dreams at two o'clock in the morning!

"When talking about the enemy we followed the example of the adults, speaking of the enemy in a derogatory way, especially the Japanese. We learned to emphasize not only their smaller physical size, but also their lack of cleanliness, so that we would preface each time, 'Dirty little . . . ' I guess that habit was our way of dealing with the constant fear that we all felt during the war. We heard rumors in the neighborhood that the Japanese were torturing the American prisoners, and the rumors turned out to be true. They also had a propaganda program because I remember hearing a Japanese woman named 'Tokyo Rose' spreading fear and hatred on our radio. Later on in life I came to realize that the views of the government of another country were not always the same as the views of their people. Maybe those people learned the same thing about us.

"In fact, now that I think about it, our own government was always getting us confused. During the war our mortal enemies were the Germans and the Japanese, and the Russians and the Chinese were our friends. But, after the war we were told that now the Germans and the Japanese were our friends, and the Chinese and the Russians were now our enemies! Oh, oh, wait a minute, it's the early nineteen fifties, and here comes the North Koreans, our new enemy—but not the *South* Koreans—they're our friends! Of course, all of this was further complicated because we, the Irish, had always distrusted the British because of their historical abuse of the Irish. But now, as Americans we were allies and supposedly friends of the British. Ha! It's no wonder we all grew up confused as hell! Maybe that's the reason why all of us kids liked to go to the cowboy movies where the good guy always wore a white hat—that way we didn't have to be told who was the bad guy and who was good guy—we knew!

"My father's sister, Aunt Maureen, had been married to Uncle Jim McDonald. She died of kidney failure, leaving him with three young children. The kidney disease was a genetic problem for the Rossiter family. Many of my relatives were affected, and soon I was also going to have the same problem. Uncle Jim was a tough but gentle man, and soon after the death of Aunt Maureen he moved his family from Binghamton to Buffalo. He wanted to have the children near his sister, Mary Rossiter, because he couldn't handle both the family and his job on the railroad. His children were Jim, Jr., Maureen and Kathy. Not only was he a good father, but he also became like a father to all of us kids on the street. We all liked Uncle Jim because he had a quiet way about him. As a young man, he had served in the army during the First World War and went into battle against the Germans in France. His oldest son Jimmy volunteered for the army in nineteen forty-two. Ironically, Jimmy also ended up fighting against the Germans in France just twenty-six years after his dad had fought there. I often wondered what thoughts were on Uncle Jim's mind during those days of the Second World War. After all, his generation was told by the government leaders that the First World War would end all wars forever. I wonder what he was thinking as he watched his son, his nephews and all the other boys on our street go off to fight a war in France where he himself had seen action just a couple of decades before? Uncle Jim suffered through two world wars, a depression in the nineteen thirties, and then the early death of his wife. In spite of all his troubles, no matter what, he kept his thoughts to himself. That's just the way it was with his generation."

-CHAPTER THREE-

ALL ABOUT OUR FAMILY

Uncle Jim was the kind of person you liked right away. He spoke very few words, and he always listened carefully whenever a young person asked him a question. He had rugged good looks, with dark, deep-set eyes that had little lines that flared out when he smiled at you. His teeth were bright white, and he had thick, black crew-cut hair with just a little gray in it. We never heard him swear or take the Lord's name in vain. In fact he always used the expression, "Gol-durnit" as a substitute for curse. He was known in the neighborhood as a religious, God-respecting man, and he never remarried after the death of Aunt Maureen. Uncle Jim wasn't a very tall man, only about five feet nine, but he was one of the most important people in my life because he helped me to feel safe during the war. In fact, for most of the kids on our street, Uncle Jim took the place of the grandfathers we had never known.

Mary Rossiter, Uncle Jim's older sister, lived exactly halfway between the McDonald home and our home. She was married to my dad's uncle, Joe Rossiter. They had four sons and one daughter, Irene. Joe Junior served in the Marines during the war, while Phil and Tom served in the army. Johnny, the oldest boy, attended the seminary during the war, preparing to become a Catholic Priest. In those days, all young boys were referred to by adding an "e" sound to their name, so they became known as Joey, Philsie, Johnny and Tommy. I was known as Jackie, and my brother was known as Mikey. This was a friendly custom meaning that you were one of the boys—accepted. Actually, my name is John, but everyone called me Jackie so people on the street wouldn't be confused. My cousin

Johnny and I were both named after our great grandfather. Joey, a
real tough guy, was the first to volunteer for the military; he went
into the Marines in the summer of nineteen forty-two. Phil and
Tom, the twins, enlisted in the army at the end of that year. When
the three Rossiter boys went off to fight in the war, Aunt Mary,
like the other mothers on our street, had three small stars displayed
on a piece of cloth in her living room window. This was a patriotic
way to signify her role as a "Gold Star Mother," which was a term
of honor. But I could tell that she was really worried about her
sons, just like all the other moms on the street. The fathers had the
same worries, but all the men tried to cover up their fear.

The bad news in those days came in the infamous telegram
from "The War Department" that began with the words: "We
regret to inform you . . ." There were three categories of news that
could be listed on the telegram: "Wounded in Action"; "Missing
in Action"; and the most terrible one, "Killed in Action." Nobody
liked to talk about someone receiving a telegram, but the news
spread rapidly through the neighborhood when a telegram came
to anyone's home. All of us were affected, young people and old
people alike. We always knew the young man involved. Many times
the telegram was about the older brother, cousin, uncle or father
of one of our friends. The sad news hurt everybody in the
neighborhood. We weren't just neighbors . . . we were family.

When my mom was working downtown, my aunt Mary would
tell me to come into her house as I was passing by on the way
home from school. She'd make me a peanut butter and jelly
sandwich in her "pantry," and then she'd ask me questions about
my schoolwork. After that she would read the letters from the
boys. At that age, such far away and mysterious-sounding places
like North Africa, Italy, The Solomon Islands, Luzon and Corregidor
fascinated me. When she read the letters, I felt very important
because I was learning so much about the world. She would spread
the big world map out on the kitchen table to show me the area
where the boys were. She said they couldn't say exactly where they
were because of the need for military secrecy. Wow! Military secrecy!
Boy, now that made me feel really important. For a young boy,

that big world out there was a place of wonder and fascination, but because so many of our young men were being killed, my feelings were mixed with worry about my cousins. There were times when Aunt Mary would read something that would make her cry, but those were things that I didn't understand then. "Are you okay, Aunt Mary?"

"Yes Jackie, I'm okay. It's just that I'm so scared and worried about the boys. Thank God you and Mikey are too young for the war. I'll just be thankful when it's over so the boys can come home."

Sometimes, my cousin Johnny would come home from the seminary while I was at the house, and I'd hear him say those magical words: "Come on Jackie, let's find some of the guys and play some football on the street." In time, I realized that playing football was Johnny's way of taking his mind off his worry about his brothers. The adults were really good at not letting their fears show. We never realized that the adults were just as scared as we were. And thank God we never found out!

Johnny was a real big hero to all the kids on the street. We looked up to him, partly because he was the only young man still around the neighborhood because of his draft exemption. He had boyish good looks, with brown eyes and blonde hair, and he loved to play football with us as much as we loved playing the game with him. He spent a lot of his free time teaching us kids how to play the game. Because Sage Avenue was a dead-end street, and because gasoline for cars was rationed, there wasn't much traffic on the street. My older brother Mikey was an altar boy, and would "serve" Mass for Johnny after he became a priest in nineteen forty-four. I went along with them to the 5:30 A.M. Mass because I wanted to be with the "big guys." We called any boy older than us a "big guy." On the way home from Mass, we stopped at Miller's Bakery for sweet-tasting "hot cross buns." We put water on the brown bag so it wouldn't catch on fire, and then put the bag into the oven to warm the buns. That was our version of the microwave oven.

Back then I thought a priest was some mysterious person who had all the answers about heaven and hell. I probably got that idea from attending Saint Bridget's grammar school, where if you didn't behave in a heavenly manner you caught holy hell from the nuns and priests. In those days all the religious people had absolute authority in the minds of our parents—especially a nun armed with a board pointer going one on one with a young boy out in the hallway! The order of nuns was named Mercy but we called them "NO-mercy nuns." There was an unspoken blind obedience and respect for the authority of the religious on the part of just about everybody—especially the parents. That tradition was a carryover from the "old country." Another reason was because most of us couldn't afford the cost of a college education before the "G.I. Bill" came along after the end of the war. And so, we were easily intimidated by anyone in a position of authority.

Quietly. That's the word which best describes the way the adults conducted their lives. Whether it was going about the daily routine of their jobs even though they were worried about the war, or the way they kept their chin up when bad news came. When a member of their family was killed, wounded or missing, they kept their feelings to themselves. Every one of them had a special toughness inside, probably because of their bitter experience with the Great Depression of the nineteen thirties that helped prepare them for all the emotional stress caused by the war. And boy, could they ever describe their toughness with just a few simple words. They used to say, "The hotter the fire, the stronger the metal!" You just had to admire them.

Of course, their deep religious beliefs helped them to cope with the insecurity and turmoil that the war placed on them. They put themselves completely into the hands of God, and as a result, they were able to overcome the pain, heartache, grief and fear that they had to live with everyday. Those were the personal qualities that we young people were exposed to, and because of it we felt safe in our neighborhood.

There were lots of family parties when we'd all get together to have a good time, even with the adults sometimes. We use to put on "plays" at the McDonald home where we'd sing about three "Jap" planes being shot down by a "Yank." We also sang traditional

Irish songs about the "old country." Johnny Rossiter played the accordion and the guitar, so he would lead us in the songs. Uncle Joe had the fastest feet in South Buffalo, and he could dance the Irish jigs and reels better than anyone in the neighborhood. We always formed a circle to cheer him on. At Halloween time we'd "dunk" for apples in a big bucket filled with water. We all played card games, Parcheesi, Monopoly and Chinese checkers. In the evening, when there wasn't any school, we played chase, tag, Relieveieo and red light green light on the street. Sometimes we just sat out on someone's front porch, or on the curb under a streetlight while we talked about our hopes and dreams for the future. In the winter we had snowball fights, went ice skating at Cazenovia "Caz" Park, and we built "forts" in the snow banks on the street.

There was an old widow named Jenny O'Malley who lived alone in the "flat" up above us. (For some unknown reason, a rental unit in those old houses was called a flat—upper or lower flat.) Mrs. O'Malley would throw a dime to me from the upstairs porch, and tell me, "Jackie, run down to Sullivan's Store and get me a quart of Ballantines Ale, and you can keep the penny change. Now remember, that's the green bottle with the three X's on the label. See Mister Sullivan—he'll know." I always had a hard time making up my mind about which candy to buy with the penny, and that made Mister Sullivan pretty anxious, but he tried to not let it show.

My dad told me that Mrs. O'Malley's husband died from lung disease back in the nineteen thirties. He got the disease when he was a "scooper" in the grain mills. A scooper is a real hard job where you use a big shovel to "scoop" the grain in the cargo hold of Great Lakes ships, or in the grain mills. It was a dangerous job because accidents happened, and you could be buried alive under tons of grain. Many of the men also got lung disease from breathing in the dust from the huge piles of grain. There were quite a few men with the nickname "Scoop" in South Buffalo, and they were always coughing. Mrs. O'Malley's only son was killed in nineteen forty-two while fighting against the Japs at a place called Bataan in the Pacific. Dad said that Mrs. O'Malley was alone and heartbroken—a word that I heard many times during the war.

And that was just around the time I got into my very first fight. One day I heard Phil O'Brien, an ignorant boy from another street, saying something about Mrs. O'Malley and me: "Hey Rossiter, I hear yer the lackey delivery boy for that old lush, Jenny O'Malley." I came home with a black eye, but O'Brien lost his front teeth. Mom and Dad didn't want me to be fighting, but they said this time it was okay. Dad smiled and whispered in my ear, "As long as the other guy looks worse than you do, Jackie!"

Like so many people in the neighborhood, my mom and dad were very aware of their Irish history and customs. Mom grew up in a big family on a small farm near Saint John's, Newfoundland. She told us lots of stories about how life could be tough there, especially in the winter. They even had two horses to pull the plow and the family buggy. When she was only twenty-one, she came to America for a better opportunity, and she came to Buffalo because an old family friend lived here. It must have been pretty scary for a young woman to leave home in those days. When I was a young boy she worked as a waitress at a downtown restaurant. Her pay was twenty-five cents an hour, plus a small amount of tips. She spent every penny on the family's food and clothes. You know, we were all poor, but we didn't realize it because everyone else in our neighborhood was also poor. We all got along well in the family because poverty has a way of making you defensive and protective of each other. It seems that it's when families have more money than they need that they become jealous of each other. Since nobody in the neighborhood had more than they needed there wasn't any jealousy between the neighbors either.

My dad came to this country to be with his uncle Joe, and to try to find a job. He had all sorts of jobs, including being a laundry deliveryman, truck driver, seaman on a Great Lakes freighter, and finally a city bus driver. His education was not much more than grade school level, but he had learned common sense at the "University of the Streets," as he would say. He had natural ability with basic math, and his penmanship was excellent. Like so many of his friends, he had a sharp awareness of Irish history, and was fiercely democratic. He also had acquired a sense of what constituted fair play, especially the treatment of people by either the government or a large corporation. Even in boxing, a sport that he followed closely, he was always pulling for "the guy in the dark trunks"— the underdog.

In nineteen forty, while working at the bus company, he and three other drivers tried to start a union. They had seen examples of what they thought was unfair labor practice and mistreatment of the workers. The company immediately labeled the men as "troublemakers" and then fired them. For the next three months, Dad had only part-time work while hearing the outspoken worry from Mom.

"Mike, how could you do such a thing when we have all these young children to feed and clothe?"

He remained silent and worried through those months of no security. A steady job meant much more than just making a living; it had to do with your identity as a man. A full-time job was almost sacred because it gave a person their sense of worth. Many times I would hear people say, "You have to earn your keep." It was agony for him to watch his friends go off to work each day.

Then came the day when he was notified to return to his full-time job as driver on the Seneca Street route. The union had been voted in by the workers following a strike, and one of the conditions for ending the strike was reinstatement of the four men—with full back pay! Also, the four men were declared "Charter Members" and given gold lifetime membership in the union, "The Amalgamated Associated Motor Coach and Streetcar Conductors of America." From that point on, their union dues would be waived for their entire life. I can still recall how Dad would show us his gold union card, and how proud he was of it. Dad had been vindicated, and he remained proud for the rest of his life that he had played a part in a small group that stood up for "the guy in the dark trunks."

Living in a predominantly Irish neighborhood had its advantages and disadvantages. A special closeness existed between people because of our commonality that's seldom seen anymore. In our case we were all Irish, all poor, and all Catholic. Most of us lived for many years on the same street—in the same neighborhood. We went to the same churches, schools and movie theaters. We listened to the same radio programs (Yes, radio programs—this was before television.) and we hung out at the same street corners and soda fountains. We had a close community feeling at all levels, such as same street, same parish and same school. Above that basic level we were all South "Bufflo" Irish. (Buffalo was always pronounced without the "a," a habit that still continues today.) What I remember most fondly about those days was the deep sense of belonging—a special feeling that came from sharing common background and common experiences. The war actually intensified those feelings, and as a result we became even more protective of each other. We were family—it was part of our identity.

The downside was that we knew very little about the people in other parts of the city, such as the Italians and the Polish. Their situation created the same reasons for bonding as ours did, and probably contributed to their lack of knowledge about us. We all tended to stay in our own neighborhoods, and our lack of knowledge about each other became our ignorance, which in turn led to distrust and friction between different ethnic groups. When we start to believe that perception is reality, it can create so many problems in life. (Ironically, what had actually been happening was that the wealthy people were playing poor ethnic groups off against each other by having them bid against each other for any available work.) The scenario was that if an Irish worker would accept, let's say twenty-five cents an hour to do a hard-labor job, then would an Italian or Polish person be willing to accept less to do the same job? Then come back to the Irish laborer for a still lower bid, continuing the vicious cycle of exploitation. It was actually much more sophisticated and subtle than the example used, but nonetheless it was a fact of life for the "blue-collar," working-class people.

The war marked the beginning of a change in our attitudes about people from other backgrounds because all of us learned that if we were going to defeat the enemy, we would have to work closely together. This meant that trust and cooperation would be needed between individuals. The close living quarters of military life brought firsthand knowledge of each other so that our ignorance began to be replaced with understanding. It's always easier to dislike someone from a distance, but it's much more difficult to dislike people after you get to know them on a personal level. It was a terrible way to achieve something so positive, but I guess some good can come from any bad experience—even something as terrible as that war.

Before my cousins went away to the war, we used to take one day every summer to visit Time's Beach and Grove near Lake Erie. All the families would ride on a big bus that the adults had rented for the day, and we were allowed to bring some friends. Of course, I always invited my best friends, Fisty Mullaney and DJ Corrigan. Fisty was three years older than DJ and me, but he didn't mind, and besides, we liked being around "big guys."

We spent the whole day swimming, playing baseball and eating hot dogs until our stomachs hurt. We must have had forty or fifty people on that old bus, and the ride home was really the best part of the whole day because everyone joined in the singing. There were "Three cheers for the conductor"; "It's a long way to Tipperrary"; "Don't sit under the apple tree"; "When Johnny comes marching home again"; and so many, many more . . . all the way home. But, then the war started . . .

-CHAPTER FOUR-

DON'T TELL DAD

Everyone knew! If you did ANYTHING, good or bad, it became known all over the neighborhood within a few hours or a few days. Everyone knew everyone else because people lived on the same street for most of their lives. We were on a first-name basis with all of the neighbors as well as their kids. Everyone attended the same churches, shopped at the same small stores, and sometimes worked at the same factories. Many of the men "stopped in" at the same bars on their way home from work. Most people couldn't afford a telephone, so people would just "stop by" for a visit. Sitting on the front porch was a favorite pastime, and this custom was especially true on our street because, being a dead-end street there was very little traffic. Neighbors would say hello from their porch as people walked past on their way home. Cars were not in such widespread use as they are today, so people did a lot more walking. For all of those reasons, if you did anything wrong your father would find out from the neighbors, from the cop on the beat, the priest or the nun, the store owner, your teacher, or the other men stopping in on the way home. News spread rapidly through the neighborhood "on the grapevine." Now the seven most dreaded words a young boy could hear were: "Wait 'til your father hears about this!"

Sister Mary's eyes were red with anger as she said those seven words that could strike fear in the heart of a young boy.

"But Sister, I REALLY couldn't help what happened. It was an accident!" She stared sternly at me as she said, "You're only going to make this matter worse by not telling me the truth, Jackie Rossiter! And that would be a mortal sin." Now I knew that it would be only a venial sin, but I wasn't about to try correcting her. She was really good at intimidating me with her authoritarian demeanor. Still, I had to plead my case.

"But Sister, I am telling the truth. It WAS an accident."

"THAT'S A MORTAL SIN."

I could sense that no amount of pleading was going to work, that she would never believe that I had peed on that other boy in the lavatory by accident. Besides, how could I tell a *NUN* that it was partly because of my kidney problem? I was ashamed to talk to anyone about such matters. After all, isn't that why we were taught to call that area our "privates?" Now I could just imagine how my "private" secret might get out and around the neighborhood if I used that as my defense. I'd be ruined! My friends would laugh and laugh for weeks. My enemies would probably tell all those silly *girls*, and that would be the worst if *girls* were laughing about my private secret.

There's no way I could ever mention that problem. NO way! I guess I'll just have to take my lumps and hope Dad doesn't find out. He'd probably kill me! I know what I'll do! I'll try to get my mom into this one, and pray that Dad doesn't find out. Moms always know what to do. Thank God that I could think fast under pressure. And thank God for our moms, because they always believed their own children to be just one step away from sainthood.

"Now, young man, you take this note home to your father right now!"

I was going to mention that it was still two hours before the end of the school day, but she was eyeballing me from behind that big oak desk in her office. The little gold-framed glasses that were always resting at the bottom of her big, sharp nose magnified her beady little eyes. She had brought me to her office by dragging me all the way from the boy's lavatory. My wrist was still sore and red from that, and besides, I didn't want any more whipping on the back of my legs, just below my short pants. She knew exactly where the tender skin was located on the back of the legs, just above the knees. Since my legs were still stinging I could only answer, "Yes, Sister," and retreat out of the school as fast as possible.

It was a nice sunny spring day, and since there wasn't anyone at home yet I decided a visit to "Caz" park on the way home was a good idea. I could go over to the creek where I was always fishing near "The Old Log" and take some time to figure out what my next strategy was going to be. Besides, I always liked being alone, especially when I was near the creek. Well, *big* mistake. I'd been sitting there for only five minutes when the notorious motorcycle cop, Mickey Dillon, pulled up and demanded to know what I was doing out of school, "playing hooky." It seemed that there was always some big shot adult around just waiting to pounce on a young boy. My heart rate was only just beginning to slow down to normal after the confrontation with Sister Mary when this big bozo jumps all over me. Well, I had no choice but to show him my leg welts and explain that the Sister had disciplined me, then sent me home to tell my parents. I was hoping for some sympathy from this cop.

"Tell them what?" He stared at me with suspicion.

"Oh, just that I misbehaved in school." I was careful not to say my name or mention my father, because I was certain that Mickey and my father probably knew each other. That would mean really catching hell, not to mention having to explain what I was doing in the park during school hours.

"Okay, but you'd better get yer butt on home soon!"

With that he revved up the motorcycle and roared away. Wow, lucky! He must have felt sorry for me because of the whip marks, and of course my innocent-looking, eight-year-old face. That cop was so mean that he'd sit at an expiring parking meter on Seneca Street for five minutes waitin' for the sixty minutes to finally run out, all the while writing up the parking ticket. We called him "Pencil Dillon" because every year he'd write more traffic tickets than anyone else on the whole police force. And little did I realize then that he'd be after me again in just a few months' time. Well, anyway, I decided I'd better get on home before I got into any more trouble.

The skeleton key was in the usual place under the mat on the front porch, and that's where everyone else in the whole world hid their key too. I never could figure out why we used the key in the first place. Why heck, you could buy a skeleton key anywhere. They were all made the same way—to fit any lock, anywhere. The big "security system" was at night when we would lock the door from the inside, then turn the key to the side in the key hole so that nobody could get their skeleton key into the lock from the outside. What a laugh! We thought the whole thing was pretty comical because what in the world did we have that anyone would want to steal? My brother Mikey used to say, "If anyone broke in to rob us they'd probably feel sorry for us and maybe leave something for us!"

Mom said that wasn't very funny, and besides, the key in the lock at night was for her own peace of mind. At that age I didn't understand her anxiety about safety.

When you had marks on your legs from the nun's board pointer the first thing you had to do was get into your dungarees so your father didn't see the evidence. If he saw the marks on my legs I'd have to lay face down on the bed with my cheeks exposed for ten whacks of his strap. Our sisters would sing with glee,

"You're gonna get a lickin'! You're gonna get a lickin'!" They never got a lickin' so they thought it was all pretty funny.

My brother and I would always hear Dad say before the first blow, "The nuns are always right."

Sometimes Dad would say, "This is gonna hurt me more than you."

I never believed that one, but I wouldn't say so because I once heard Mikey say, "I doubt that!" His remark got him an extra couple of smacks even though Dad laughed at what he said.

Thank God no one was home so I could cover the evidence on my legs. The red marks on my wrist were still there, but I had it all planned out to say Fisty Mullaney bet me that he could make me say "uncle" by giving me an "Indian burn." An Indian burn was when the other guy wraps both of his hands around your wrist, and then puts pressure on the skin in opposite directions to make red marks on your arm. Anyone who yelled out in pain was judged the worst thing possible, a chicken. The only thing worse than a chicken was a squealer, also known as a ratfink. Okay, there, I've got an excuse worked out, so now I'm not so worried. Guess I'll relax with a peanut butter sandwich before I get my homework done. The rule was no homework done, no play, and I wanted to listen to the radio serials from five to six o'clock before supper. There were four fifteen-minute programs: Buck Rogers, Tom Mix, Jack Armstrong, The All-American Boy, Superman and Sky King. Those programs alternated with Straight Arrow, Comanche Warrior, Dick Tracy, and The Green Hornet. Listening to your favorite radio program was just like reading a good book because you used your imagination to form a picture of the action in your mind. That way, in your mind you could become really involved in the story.

Mikey came home first and wanted to know why I was home ahead of him, and where I got that red mark on my arm.

"I ran all the way home, and Fisty tried to make me yell uncle with an Indian burn."

"Bull! You can't run that fast, Jackie. Who you kiddin'?"

"I can so, and besides, I didn't want Fisty to hear me cry when my arm started to burn." I figured that last remark would throw him off the trail.

"Oh, okay. Is anyone else home yet?"

"No, I'm the first one."

"Are you gonna be listenin' to those stupid radio serials at five o'clock?"

"Yeah, I was hopin' to."

"Well, there's somethin' I wanna listen to at five. Tell ya what; I'll flip ya for it. You call it, Jackie."

"Heads. Ha—I win," I said.

"No way, best out a' three."

"You always say that if you lose on the first flip, Mikey."

Well, this was my lucky day, 'cause I won the toss on the next one too. It wasn't long before I began to fall asleep in front of our big Zenith "Super Heterodyne" radio, and as I drifted off, I heard the voice of Tom Mix singing, "Take a tip from Tom—go and tell your mom Hot Ralston can't be beat."

"Jackie. Jackie! Come on, get up, it's time for supper."

"Oh, hi, Mom. Okay, what's for supper?"

"Liver and lima beans." Oh God, I thought, not that barf food, I hate that stuff. Guess I'll have to fake goin' to the bathroom so I can spit most of it out again. I wished we were havin' mashed potatoes and roast beef, but we could afford that only once a month or so.

"Hi, Dad, how ya' doin?"

"Hi, Jackie, not bad kiddo. How ya doin'? How was school today?"

"Oh, about the same as always, Dad." "Hi, Maggie. Hi, Mo. Hi, Mare." At fourteen, Margaret was the oldest, and she was always looking out for me when Mom was working. Right away she noticed the red marks from Sister Mary pulling me down the hallway.

"Where'd you get those red marks on your wrist, Jackie?"

"Oh, it's just an Indian burn from Fisty Mullaney."

I watched cautiously out of the corner of my eye to see if Dad was listening. He looked but didn't say anything, so I breathed a sigh of relief, figuring I was in the clear for now. Then I got really relaxed when he said that because of some big event downtown he'd have to work on Sunday. Great, I thought, that way I can explain everything to Mom on Sunday, and instead of Dad, she could go down to see Sister Mary at school.

"Where you goin', Jackie?"

I mumbled to Dad that I had to go to the bathroom.

"Well, you make sure you come right back here and finish your dinner."

After I spit that awful stuff into the toilet and came back to the table, he watched me with suspicion as I toyed around with the food on my plate. "You make sure you eat everything on your plate, Jackie; your eyes are always bigger than your belly. Do you know how many people are starvin' in Africa?" I wondered where the heck Africa was, and whether those kids had to eat lima beans and liver?

"Mom, can I go to the movies at the Orpheum tomorrow? There's twenty-five cartoons and the Flash Gordon serial playin'."

"How much does it cost, Jackie?"

"Eight cents, and ya even get a box a' popcorn free!"

Dad said, "We'll see, but right now you've gotta finish everything on that plate."

Oh God, he's still watchin' my plate. Now what'll I do? I told myself just hold yer nose, grit yer teeth and get it down—otherwise no movies. Boy, the things a kid had to do just to go and see a movie. I wonder if the kids in Africa have to go through all this just to see a movie?

"All right, you little punks! If you dummies don't stop throwin' things at the screen we'll cancel the movie and kick all of ya' out!" The usher's attitude was defiant as he stood in the middle of the stage after they had turned off the projector and stopped Flash Gordon cold in his tracks.

"Booooo!"

"Hey, maybe we got a better idea: We could get officer Dillon down here, lock all the doors except one, and he could take all your names down and tell your fathers." This threat started a murmur of subdued whispering. "Ok, now ya' little creeps, so shut up or that's the next move!" As the lights went off and the movie came back on there were a few hand made "raspberries," but the usher ignored it.

"Hey, Fisty, did you see the size of that rat just ran down the aisle?"

"Aw, DJ, that wasn't a rat—it was Pencil Dillon lookin' fer ye'r old man."

"Bull!" Hell on you man, it was a big, fat rat!"

I said, "No, really, I saw it too. It was a real big rat!"

"What the hell's wrong with you sissies, haven't ya' ever seen a rat before?"

We both answered together, "Not in here we haven't!"

"Au kiss off—I've seen rats here lotsa' times."

DJ said, "Malarkey, yer full of it, Fisty."

"You callin' me a liar, carrot top?" Referring to DJ's bright red hair.

I said, "Au, come on you guys, there's enough fightin' already with the war and everything—cut it out."

"Hey, you little jerks, shut up in there!" The usher was shining his light on us. "If you guys don't shut up, yer out a' here."

Fisty said, "Au, stuff it, bellhop," referring to the usher's uniform.

Out we went into the alleyway behind the movie house. "And stay the hell out of here ya little micks!"

"Damn, why'd ya' have ta go and get us kicked out like that, Fisty?"

"Oh, kiss off Rossiter! Besides, that movie stunk. How ridiculous can ya' get? Three guys landin' a rocket ship on the moon! That couldn't happen in a million years."

DJ said, "Hey, I got an idea—let's go hoppin' garages!"

Now that's one thing that we could all agree on. "ALL RIGHT!"

The garages on the streets were laid out back to back in a checkerboard pattern. The idea was to see how many garages you could jump to without touching the ground. If you missed and hit the ground in between, you were out of the game, and the last man out was the winner. My nickname was "The Monkey" because I usually won the garage-jumping contest, and I could climb to the highest part of a Chestnut tree to get the best Chestnuts to play "Kingers" in the schoolyard. This time DJ won the garage-jumping contest, and on the way home we stopped for a foot-long, penny pretzel at Sullivan's delicatessen. We talked about the coming summer and how we could go swimmin', fishin', camping out and playin' baseball down at the end of our street in our secret place we called, "The Field." The more we talked about the summer the more excited we became. We could hardly wait.

"Hey," I said, "look over there—it's the iceman!" The iceman was delivering big blocks of ice to the houses on the street for what we called our "icebox"—the place where we kept our food. This was just before the days of the refrigerator, and we all had to have ice delivered to keep our food cold. Since there was seldom any money available for candy, one of our treats was to get a big piece of ice to suck on.

Fisty said, "Ok, let's wait for him to take a block of ice into Jimmy McCarthy's house, then we can snatch some." The iceman would have given us a chunk if we asked, but we liked the challenge of "stealing" it—that was more fun. We made off with our prize and then sat on the front porch with Jimmy McCarthy. We liked to listen to Jimmy tell us spooky stories about the boy that stole the old man's liver, and how the old man's ghost would come back to the boy's house at three o'clock in the morning looking for his lost liver. It seems that every spooky story happened at three o'clock in the morning. Fisty said that's because they closed all the bars at that time.

"Johnny, I'm on the first step . . . Johnny I'm on the second step . . . " Jimmy was four years older than us, and he sometimes used words that we didn't always understand. One day Jimmy used the dreaded "F" word, and so when I went home I decided to use it in front of my mother. I didn't have a clue about what the word meant.

"What was that word you said, Jackie?" Her facial expression was one of shock.

"What? What word, Ma?" Her tone of voice began to make me feel guilty, but I didn't know why I felt that way.

"I'm gonna wash your mouth out with soap!" She then stuck a bar of "Fels-Naptha" brown soap way back into my mouth, rubbing it back and forth against my teeth. Oh God, what a rotten taste!

"Don't you EVER use that word again, do you hear?" *She was really emphatic.*

"What word, Ma?" Her eyelids squinted down and her jaw tightened up, making her lips appear smaller. She was really mad.

"Never mind now, just don't you EVER say that again!"

"But, what word, Ma?" She was reluctant to say the actual word. Her voice intensified with authority as she snapped, "That 'F' word!"

"Why not, Mom?"

"Look, Jackie, don't try my patience by askin' any more questions, or you'll be getting yer mouth washed out again, understand?"

Her dark red hair seemed to be standing on end and her freckles were glowing because she was so mad. I decided I better not ask any more questions. She was so upset by that dumb-sounding word though, that it got my curiosity up. I decided that someday I'd have to ask Jimmy McCarthy what that word meant . . . "Well now, nooo kiddin', Jimmy, so THAT'S what it means, huh . . . Wow!" And that's the way most of us obtained that part of our education back then—on the streets and misinformed.

On Sunday, after Dad left for work I told Mom about the note from Sister Mary, and how I was supposed to bring Dad with me before I could come back to school.

"Oh, my God, Jackie, how did that happen? You didn't pee on that boy on purpose now, did you?"

"Oh, no Mom, but how could I tell a nun about my private secret?"

"Private secret? What are you talkin' about, Jackie?"

"Well, you know, about what you told me when you said I was born at home, not in the hospital."

"Oh, you mean about the possibility that you might have a kidney problem?"

"Yeah—that's it!"

"You're not lyin' about that being the reason for what happened now, are you, Jackie?"

"I swear to God that's the reason, Ma. Cross my heart and hope to die!"

"Well, okay then, I'll go in and talk to Sister Mary about it in the morning."

"But remember, Mom, we can't let my secret get out or all the kids will laugh at me!"

When Mom mentioned the need for confidentiality to Sister Mary that Monday morning, the both of them became involved in a heated discussion.

"Really, Mrs. Rossiter, just what do you think I am, a gossip?"

"Sister, now let's not be readin' anything into my request, other than what it is—simply a request! And by the way Sister, if you had taken at face value what Jackie had said about this being an accident perhaps this meeting would not have been necessary, and I would not have lost precious time from my work to come here."

I was careful not to show any facial expression, but I was thinking, "Wow, way to go, Mom!"

"Well, Mrs. Rossiter, perhaps we should refer this problem over to Monsignor Foley."

"Now that's a fine idea, Sister Mary, as I'm quite sure that the good Monsignor would certainly be able to understand a *man's* problem such as this!"

The nun thought carefully for a few minutes before saying, "Well, we wouldn't want to bother the Monsignor—after all, his time is so valuable to the needs of the parish."

Mom was not about to lose her advantage. "As is my time to the needs of my family, Sister."

The meeting ended with Mom having the upper hand. Before I went back to class though, she whispered to me, "Now you watch yourself from here on, Jackie; she'll be spoilin' for revenge, so you'd best be keepin' yer nose clean. Do you understand my meanin', son?"

"Yeah, Mom. See ya' at suppertime. And thanks!"

As time went by, I began to realize that my mother had not only put the Sister on the defensive, she had also put me on notice not to get into any more trouble in the future. After the experience of having to deal with Mom, if there were a next time, Sister Mary would certainly want to talk only to Dad. And I wanted no part of that! Now wouldn't ya' know it, the next day DJ and Fisty wanted me to skip school with them and hide up in the loft in DJ's garage.

"I don't know, guys, that's a lot'a fun but I'm still on 'guard duty' now (That's watchin' out for adults because they're watchin' you), and I don't want any more trouble with Sister Mary right now."

Fisty said, "Hey, yeah, how come ya peed on that kid anyway, Jackie?"

"Au, he was callin' me names like 'Mick', and other stuff like that." I lied because I didn't want to start talkin' about my private problem.

"He called you a 'Mick'—so what in the heck is he?"

"I dunno, maybe Italian or somethin'." Sometimes one lie follows another.

"Well, hell on him then, let's go whip his butt real good!"

"Holy cow! No, no, we can't do that 'cause that would get me into a real mess with Sister and my dad." Now if there were anyone Fisty was afraid of, for some unknown reason that would be MY father. Come to think of it, I was really afraid of HIS father.

"Yer dad himself, Jackie? Damn, he's hell on wheels when he gets mad. That's what my old man says. Maybe yer right, Jackie, we better leave that guy alone, at least fer now anyway."

-CHAPTER FIVE-

THE FUN OF SUMMERTIME!

The last few weeks of the school year dragged on painfully slow; the days in school always seemed so much longer as we got closer to summer recess. Playing stickball and Kingers in the schoolyard helped to pass the time. Stickball could be played with as few as two boys, and if you hit the ball a certain pre-agreed upon distance, it could count as anything from a single to as much as a home run. The problem always came with the difference of opinion about how far the ball had traveled.

"It's only a triple, Rossiter!"

"No, it's not, DJ, it's definitely a home run!"

"Oh yeah, well yer blind, Jackie boy."

"Yeah, well yer loony tunes, Danny boy!"

"Ah, so's yer old man!"

On the way home from school, Fisty always wanted to yell at the drunks hanging out in Murphy's bar and grill. Murphy's had swinging doors just like in the western movies, so we'd stick our heads under the doors and yell, "Barflies! Barflies!" Then we'd run like hell down an alleyway between the houses, hop the fences, and then cut back to Seneca Street. Fisty said he liked to do it just for the fun of it, but we knew it was probably because he didn't like his own dad hanging out in bars after his workday was done on the railroad. Well, anyway, exams were finally finished, and we all squeaked by with a passing grade. Now it was time to head over to "The Old Log" at Caz Park for fishin' and swimmin'. Yeah!

Cazenovia Park was laid out just right for the adventures of young boys. Much later on in life I learned that a famous designer,

Fredrick Law Olmstead, had designed Caz. Olmstead had designed and built several parks in Buffalo during the industrial boom of the nineteenth century, at a time when the city was home to many wealthy families. He had also built other now-famous parks, including Central Park in New York City. Of course, at that age those facts didn't have much interest for me because I was much too occupied with enjoying the famous man's handiwork.

The park was a sprawling mass of green play space covering much of South Buffalo. It bordered the south edge of the city, and beyond was mostly countryside and farms back then—before the start of the suburbs. Since the southern boundary simply blended into the rural countryside, the park gave you a feeling of being "out in the country."

There were three professionally styled baseball fields in a large area that was dug out, so that spectators could sit on the grassy slopes running about twenty feet up from the playing fields. This tiered effect of the seating on the grass sloping up from the playing field meant that all of the fans could easily see play on the field. There was a large swimming pool complex, with first-class, Olympic-style swimming and diving pools, as well as a wading pool. The wading pool was fun because there was a big fountain in the middle. Nearby was a big food and beverage casino.

The most southerly part of the park contained a nine-hole golf course. Since golf was a game thought then to be a pastime for people of the upper class, and due to the high cost of the equipment needed, we didn't know any of the people who used the course. We did, however, sometimes volunteer to recover any balls "lost" in the creek—for a ten-cent fee of course. By giving some of the balls a little extra help with our foot, we always made sure there were plenty of "lost" balls to dive for.

Meandering through the middle of the park was the focal point—Cazenovia Creek. The creek was relatively shallow, being just a few feet deep with small rapids in some places, and pool areas of about eight feet deep in other places. Mature willow trees lined the banks in most areas, and where the water was deep enough for wading there were small sandy spots for sunbathing. Every summer a six-foot dam was erected to form deep areas on most parts of the creek, giving the park a look of peaceful tranquility.

On the west side of the creek, there was a very large pond set off by itself, which was used for ice skating in the winter, and bank-side fishing in the summer. The overflow from the pond went into the creek and was controlled by a mini dam located under a stone bridge near the creek. The stone bridge served as a meeting place, as well as a place for various kids' games like Relieveieo. It was a good fishing spot to catch Rock Bass and Sunfish, which we called "Sunnies." Later on I learned that it was also a favorite spot for the "big guys" to shoot dice.

Running through the park from east to west was Cazenovia Parkway, a lightly traveled curving road with a bridge across the creek. Because of the color of the bridge we always called it the "Green Bridge." About one hundred yards south of the Green Bridge was the most fun and legendary place of all our dreams: "The Old Log." "The Old Log" had a magical effect on us. Just the mention of that place could start us daydreaming. There was a long, knotted rope hanging from one of the many big willow trees that we used to swing (naked) into the eight-foot-deep water. It was where we also fished for so many hours to catch Suckers and Black Bass. But the real meaning of that place was so much more to us boys: For us it was more of a state of mind, a secret place where we went with only our very best friends. The entire Cazenovia Park was our favorite place to go to as boys, but only "The Old Log" could still stir up magical memories for all of us—even after the passing of fifty-five years.

Armed with plenty of "night crawlers" caught the night before, we usually started fishing around eight in the morning. Around noon, we'd take all our clothes off and dive in off "The Old Log." The water was usually pretty dirty, but this was early June, and the public pool didn't open until the first of July. We just couldn't wait that long to start swimmin'.

"Did everyone keep yer clothes near the creek bank, and hide yer fishin' gear in case Pencil Dillon shows up? Yeah? Okay then, last one in's a girl!"

"Pencil Dillon" was a famous motorcycle cop who would always show up to chase us out of the water because he said it was "against the law." Now that creek had raw sewage floating downstream, water rats, snapping turtles, water snakes and salamanders, so the least of our worries was that dumb cop. But, every time we got into the water, as sure as God made little green apples, Dillon would come speeding through the park to order us, "Out of the water!" We figured that guy must have built-in radar, and sure enough this time, "Watch out, here comes Dillon!"

He came through the park from the opposite side as usual, so we swam over to the creek bank on the other side. To get our attention he would accelerate his motorcycle, "Vroom! Vroom!" He did that same routine every time he came there.

"All right, you little punks, get the hell out a' that water!"

That's about the time when we'd start the mockery: Artificial farts, indecent gestures, mooning and other derogatory comments.

"Kiss off, Dillon!" "Fatso!" "Yer granny wears combat boots."

Of course, we were in the clear on the other side of the creek, so we had plenty of courage. Then, when he'd race up to the green bridge to cross over and come down on our side, we'd simply hold our rolled-up clothes over our heads while we dog paddled to the other creek bank. Then the entire scenario would be repeated once more until he'd finally leave in frustration. Sometimes we figured that it was just as much of a game to him as it was for us.

"I'll catch you little punks someday!"

After he left, we had to take turns keepin' a lookout because sometimes he'd park his motorcycle somewhere and try to sneak up on us. After a swim we'd get back to fishin' for Black Bass, Suckers and Bullheads. While we were waiting for a fish to bite we usually talked about all kinds of stuff.

"Hey Jackie, remember that time you saw an article in that magazine about how you could get lots of worms out of the ground by riggin' up the electric on yer lawn? I thought yer old man was gonna have a conniption fit that night!"

"Holy smokes, DJ, it's a wonder we didn't kill ourselves when that big flash and spark went off in the wet lawn."

Fisty said, "What a couple a' jerks; don't know diddly about short circuits and all that kinda 'lectric stuff."

DJ said, "Yeah, well you weren't so smart about that stuff till his dad told us."

I said, "How the heck was I supposed to know ya couldn't put both the wires on one metal rod?"

Fisty said, "Damn, Jackie, don't ya remember 'bout Ben Franklin and that kite story stuff in school?"

"Nah, I figured that was just a buncha malarkey, anyway."

DJ said, "Hey, baseball season's here, how's about we go down to the field tomorrow? Besides, Dillon's mad as hell now, so we better lie low for a while."

"Good idea, but we better watch out for the Polaks from Kaisertown on other side of the river. My brother Mikey and the other big guys said the Polaks made a raid on their fort yesterday."

Fisty said, "Big deal, we'll just throw some rocks at 'em. My old man says that's how they took care a' the Protestants in Ireland when he was a kid."

"Yeah, but that's 'cause the Catholics didn't have any guns, right? Hey, speakin' about guns, my brother Mikey says the Polaks have BB guns now, so watch out!"

DJ spoke for all of us when he said, "Oh boy, I wish I could have one of those lever-action BB guns. They look just like the saddle guns those cowboys have in the flicks. But my mom says no way, it'd just get me into more trouble with the Polaks when I'm in too deep already."

I said, "Yeah, my mom said the same thing, but then I started askin' about how maybe could I have one of those 'Whammo' slingshots like I saw in a magazine one time.

"So she says, 'That's the same idea, and now who do you think you are this time, David in the Bible maybe?'" Fisty said, "Hey, you guys know ya can make a slingshot from a tree branch shaped like a Y, then use a piece a' rubber inner tube tied to each side of the Y. I saw a big guy with one, and I'm gonna make one just like it."

I said, "Oh, oh, look out! Here comes Peewee Hayes and Butch Ryan; we better get the hell out a' here."

Hayes and Ryan were the local bullies, about four years older than us. They were always lookin' to beat up someone smaller than themselves. You know the type: bad teeth, lots of cavities with nicotine stains on their mouth and fingers. They always had a lit cigarette hangin' out of their mouth because they thought that was cool. They came from an area of the city we called "The Ward," a place where there were mostly "shanty" Irish, meaning very poor and very tough people. They called us "lace curtain" Irish, because they said that we had more stuff than they did. That was a laugh. Why, we even had to put cardboard in our shoes when there was a hole in the sole, until our mother could come up with the money for new shoes. When it was raining, we had to sit all day long in school with wet socks.

Butch Ryan said, "Hey, ya little dummies, we told ya ta stay the hell out a' the park, so you punks better hat up or we'll whip yer butts real good! And you Rossiter, ya little punk, I think we'll kick yer butt right now, just fer the hell of it!" I was the smallest and the skinniest of the three of us kids.

Peewee Hayes said, "Maybe we should de-pants these punks and call the girls over fer a laugh." They both started grinnin'. Fisty was startin' to get really mad.

He said, "Look jerks, yer both in OUR neighborhood now, so maybe you guys better shove off. If I can't whip ya, my brother Gerry will kick both yer butts—same time!"

Fisty was tall and rangy for his age, with long arms and big feet. He already had broad shoulders and large hands, but these bullies were even bigger than him. He could handle the mechanics of boxing as well as anyone, but his determination was really his edge before a fight even got started. The psychological edge was that Fisty had a very quiet confidence about him. I never saw him back down from a fight—and I never saw him lose a fight. He spoke very few words, but you just knew that he was willing to fight by looking into his eyes. The opposition saw this and many times they would be intimidated by his determined stare into their eyes. They knew before it ever started that "he could put up."

"Oh yeah, little punk, so who's yer freakin' brother, Superman maybe?"

"He's the golden gloves champ of all New York State, that's who, jerk!"

"Oh, yeah, well what's his name? I think yer fulla bull, kid."

DJ spoke next: "His brother's Gerry Mullaney, the boxer who kicked hell out a' Slattery, that guy from yer neighborhood, that's who!"

With the mention of that tough guy's name getting beat, their eyes began to show uncertainty for the first time, then the uncertainty slowly changed to fear.

"Hey you guys no need ta get bent out a' shape. We were only kiddin'."

Fisty smelled a chicken cookin'. "Ya' know guys, I bet I could whip these two dummies myself—that is, if I was in the mood." They both started backing up as Fisty said, "Ok, which one wants ta duke it out first?" They turned and beat it to the sound of our jeers of "Chicken!" I found enough courage to say, "And don't come back!"

I never forgot the lesson of life that I learned that day in the park: If you don't challenge a bully, he'll just keep taking advantage of you. Giving in to a bully will only encourage him to demand more and more, and then it becomes a never-ending habit. Examples of bullies were all around in those days: Hitler, Mussolini, Tojo, Stalin, etc. But, I sure had to admit that I was glad to be one of Fisty's good friends that day—and also in the years that followed. While he couldn't protect DJ and me from everything, word did get around the neighborhood if you were his friend, and that had a magical effect on other boys that didn't like you for some reason or other. The next morning, I found out that our trip to the field would have to wait because a War Department telegram came to Aunt Mary's house during the night.

It was Saturday afternoon, and all of us from the three related families went to Uncle Joe's house at 51 Sage Avenue to find out that Joe Junior was missing after a battle at a place called Solomon Islands. The Marines suspected that he had been captured, but couldn't say for sure, so that's why the telegram said "Missing in Action." All of us kids were scared and quiet while the adults talked in low voices. My mom hugged Aunt Mary as she started to cry softly.

"Now, now, Mary, there's always hope that Joe will come through this . . . He's a tough guy, always remember that."

The men were trying to find the exact location of Solomon Islands on the big map spread across the kitchen table, because that's all we had: a spot on a map somewhere on the other side of the world. I suspected that the other kids were just as scared as I was, but none of us let on about our fears that day. Only when I was alone with Fisty and DJ could I talk about my fears and bad dreams. The bad dreams were really scary that night. Mom and the girls tried to comfort Aunt Mary until Doc Carden showed up to check on her.

I heard him and my dad talking at the door. "Did someone call you, Doc?"

"No, Mike, I heard about it from some of the neighbors and I thought I might be able to help out." Doc Carden went into the dining room with Aunt Mary for a few minutes. When they came out to the kitchen Aunt Mary had stopped crying, but her eyes were still red.

"Here, Joe, this is a prescription to help her sleep, and maybe you should take one of the pills too."

"Thanks for comin' over, Doc. How much do I owe you?"

"Now, now. We'll talk about that when young Joe comes home."

Then he smiled at Uncle Joe and hugged Aunt Mary before saying goodbye. My mom and cousin Irene made some hot tea and snacks for everyone, while my sister Margaret went to O'Connell's drug store to get the prescription filled. Dad told Mikey and me that it was best if we all stayed until Uncle Joe and Aunt Mary were good and tired. We left for home at about ten, and before we left I noticed that Uncle Joe's eyes were really red and his voice was cracking when he said: "Goodnight to all of you—my very best friends."

My dad and Uncle Jim said, "We'll remember Joe in our prayers, Unc'. See ya at Mass in the mornin'."

"By now most of you have heard the news about young Joe Rossiter. Please now, I want all of you to offer up your prayers today for the safe return of one of our own. I've known Joe senior since he came to this country as a young man some forty years ago. As a matter of fact his own granddad and mine were best'a friends in the old sod at Wexford, so ya' see now we go way back. It was myself who baptized and confirmed all of the Rossiter children right here in this very church. And it's my hope that someday when Johnny takes his final vows he'll be able to come on board right here at Saint Bridget's to keep our close family ties alive . . . Mary, Joe, Irene and Johnny, may the good Lord give you all the peace of mind and spirit while we wait for the safe return of young Joe. Dear God above, watch over and protect Joseph, and his brothers Phil and Tom, who are now serving in North Africa along with young Jimmy McDonald and all the other young boys. Good Lord in heaven, sometimes it seems as if the whole world has gone insane, with war raging all around the world. Please help men of goodwill prevail, and allow our children to return home to the love of their families. In the holy name of Jesus, amen . . ."

That was the message from the pulpit at the Sunday morning Mass, and during that message we all had a difficult time controlling our emotions. That Sunday in June of 1943 was also the first time that I had ever seen Monsignor Foley so close to tears. But, that's just the way it was: When a family found themselves in "a time of trouble" as the expression went, everyone in the neighborhood would come to the aid of that family. Now little did any of us realize then, but it was going to be a very long time before we would learn the fate of Joe Junior. All during that long wait we all worried, especially Uncle Joe and Aunt Mary. Since we could see the anxiety on their faces each day, it kept Joe always in our thoughts too. And that day wouldn't be the last time we'd all be there in church, praying for our relatives in the military. During that war we all knew that trouble was always just around the corner. We were constantly under the stress of "waiting for the other shoe to drop."

In the meantime, I was having my own problems in the neighborhood with boys we called "wisenheimers." Those were the kind of kids that weren't exactly bullies; just troublemakers who tried to make you feel bad about yourself. Uncle Jim said that type of person had feelings of insecurity themselves. If they could make you feel bad about yourself it helped them to improve their own self-esteem, but only in their own minds.

"Ya see boys, it's kinda like a lifeguard tryin' ta save someone from drowning. The guy drowning grabs hold and pushes the lifeguard down to elevate himself up above the water. That's why the first thing they teach the lifeguard is how ta break all the different holds. By the way, as you go through life yer gonna find plenty a' those wisenheimers around. The trick is to ignore 'em; don't let 'em get to ya." Of course, at that age it was sometimes difficult to always follow good advice. Everyone in the neighborhood was proud of their Irish ancestry, and their family name.

"Mom, how come some of the kids in the neighborhood ask me, "What kinda name would Rossiter be? They're always sayin' that's not an Irish name. Is that true, Mom?" She tried to give me a quick answer but then saw that I was serious about wanting to know. "I don't want to be treated different, Ma."

"Well now, Jackie, come on over here to the table; sit down and we'll talk. In fact, now that I think about it, Mikey had the same trouble a few years ago, and I had to explain all of this to him. You see, Jackie, Your dad's paternal grandfather—now that would be on his father's side—immigrated to Canada from County Wexford, Ireland around the early eighteen hundreds. There had been an uprising against the British rulers by the people of Ireland because of all the bad treatment that the Irish had suffered simply because they were Catholic. The British had a regular army while the Irish were mostly farmers and fishermen armed with nothing more than farm implements, so the British were victorious very quickly. After the fighting ended, the British soldiers were extremely cruel, burning and wrecking people's property. They also confiscated the small homes and property away from the people. This was the reason why most of our ancestors, including mine, moved away to try to start a new life in Canada and Newfoundland—because they were left with little or nothing, sometimes just the clothes on their backs."

"But, Mom, what about our name?"

"Well, you see Jackie that goes way back, oh, about six hundred years earlier when the Rossiters first came to the southeast part of Ireland from Normandy, in France. They were then known as Norman people—originally from Scandinavia."

"Then it's true what the kids say about our name!"

"Well, let me explain it this way, son: Irish people are not a race, they are a collection of several different peoples, bound together by the same language, religion and customs over many hundreds of years. Being Irish is not determined by some silly technical term. Being Irish is more about what's in your heart. You see, if your family had spent over six hundred years in this country right here you would have more of a claim to being "American" than most people living here right now. So the next time one of your friends says something about your name, now you tell him this: The Rossiters lived in Ireland for over six hundred years. They spoke the Gaelic language. They shared the customs of the Irish, and they fought alongside the Irish against invaders. They shared the common hardships and happiness together. They died in Ireland and are buried all over that land. Now if that's not being Irish, I certainly don't know what is!"

"Wow, Mom, you're really smart, I didn't know you knew so much about our history."

"Jackie, if you're truly Irish you'll always know about your heritage. Now that just might be the most important part of being Irish. And Jackie, when you tell some of your friends about this, you be nice now, don't be fightin' over it. God knows there's been plenty enough a' that in the world already . . . "

"Okay, and thanks, Mom!"

-CHAPTER SIX-

KAISERTOWN AND "THE FIELD"

We called the area at the end of our street "The Field," one of those places of magic for young boys—our own secret place known only to a select few. The Field was immediately at the end of our street, protected by a chain-link fence and a sign that said, "dead end." Of course, only a very few of us knew the exact location of the "secret" hole in the fence. At least we liked to think so anyway. Beyond the fence, the field was about seventy feet or so wide, then dropping down a slope to the Buffalo River, which was about one hundred and twenty feet wide and about thirty feet deep. The field widened out to the left, behind the last houses on the street, to about three hundred feet deep, and stretching about a half-mile north along the riverbank. To the right, or south of our street, the river curved away to the southeast. Just beyond the curve was a railroad trestle located about five hundred feet from Sage Avenue. The trestle connected Irish South Buffalo with Polish East Buffalo, an area known as "Kaisertown," which was a name from the past when it had been a predominantly German neighborhood. The Irish and the Polish had mutual distrust of each other, based probably on nothing more than the way we pronounced the English language, or the differences in the type of food that we ate. We laughed at the thought of eating something as strange sounding as "kielbasa," and the Polish laughed at eating something as strange as "corned" beef and cabbage. The little things in life during those times usually caused the most trouble. Since the war was in progress, and of course all of us boys from both sides of the river were "war conscious," we probably fanaticized about being in a "state of war" with each other. I don't think any of us knew any Italian people at that time—something that wouldn't change for several more years.

In those days none of us knew very much about other ethnic groups, and what little we knew was usually from our imagination, not reality. We Irish all thought the world revolved around Ireland and the Irish. It was summed up by an expression so often heard in the neighborhood. "There's only two kinds of people in this world: Irish, and those who wish they were Irish!" That statement was most likely a reaction to over three hundred years of mistreatment of the Irish Catholics at the hands of the British. At that time we were reasserting our pride in ourselves, and we were not about to take any more abuse from anyone, anytime, anywhere! Collectively, we had a "chip on our shoulder."

The other ethnic groups probably felt the same way about themselves, I'm sure. We, all of us, were either recent immigrants, or the sons and daughters of immigrants, so we tended to band together in this new land with "our own kind"—as the expression went. This was our way of feeling secure in a relatively new country, amongst so many "foreigners." For those reasons, different sections of our city, any city in fact, was made up mostly of one ethnic group such as Polish, German, Italian, Irish, etc. Where the "turf" bordered was where the friction could usually be found, and in this case it was South Buffalo and Kaisertown.

"The Polaks are coming! The Polaks are coming!"

At that age nothing can hold a young boy's attention for very long—even something as serious as a War Department telegram. The Polish teenage boys were coming from their neighborhood of "Kaisertown" across the river located at the end of our street. We could see the BB guns in their hands as they came towards us in their canoes. I said to DJ and Fisty, "Come on, you guys, let's get out a' here real fast!"

"No way, Jackie, let's let 'em have it with these big rocks!" When Fisty's mind was made up you couldn't reason with him, and besides DJ was already letting fly with rocks at the three canoes.

"I hit the canoe! I hit the canoe," he yelled at the top of his voice. I could hear the "ping" of the BB's hitting the steel pilings where we had run for cover.

"Ya' see, guys," DJ said, "I told ya' it was a good idea ta pile up plenty a' rocks here! Ya just never know when yer gonna need ammo."

"Hey ya little Micks, we're comin' up there ta beat yer butts!"

Fisty yelled back, "Hell on you guys, that's a lot a' horse manure. Here, try this one on fer size!" With that he threw a big rock from our cover behind the steel pilings. Someone yelled out from the direction of the water,

"Holy, look out—that's a big one!" With that we got some courage and started throwing rocks from the safety of our cover, lobbing them artillery style over the top of the pilings in rapid succession.

"Damitt! Let's get the hell out a' here, there's no way we can get 'em from here!" The Polaks always said "damitt," letting the "t" sound linger on. We started taunting them as they rowed away.

"Damitt, you Polaks are really dumb!"

They yelled back as they headed for the other shore, "We'll rip yer little Mick heads off when we get a' hold a ya, damitt punks!"

We were so busy congratulating ourselves that we didn't see that they had pulled their canoes ashore and were running towards the Railroad Bridge to try to cut us off from our own street.

"Holy smokes, let's bug out a' here!"

They were trying to cut us off from getting down our street so we ran as fast as we could, with the adrenaline of fear pushing us way beyond our normal speed. We started down our street towards our own houses with them in hot pursuit and gaining.

Fisty was yelling that we should stop and "take 'em on."

I yelled back, "No way! They'll kill us. They're all big guys!"

Just then, when we thought they were about to catch us, I heard my brother's voice yell out, "Hey, what the hell are you jerks doin' in our neighborhood?"

Mikey was on Lenahan's front porch with three other big guys, and the four of them started running towards our pursuers and us. At first the Polaks only slowed up, but then began to realize they had gone too far down an Irish neighborhood street. Suddenly there were people of all different ages coming out on their porches. A father yelled out, "Hey, what the hell are you big guys doin', chasin' little kids like that?"

That's when the pursuers became the pursued. I was actually hoping that nobody would catch them because this was starting to become a "mountain out of a molehill," and besides I was getting scared at the thought of this mob getting even for something we had started. Fisty was in hot pursuit, swearing and urging on what had now become a very large "posse." "Come on, let's get the chicken Polaks, damitt punks!"

He pronounced that word just like they did. Well, thank God nobody got hurt because the same adrenaline that had helped us run fast now made the Polish boys run faster than us, and we decided to stop halfway across the railroad bridge. That was the usual practice, and besides, the other side was their neighborhood where WE would be outnumbered. At the dinner table that evening, my older sister Margaret said, "Jackie, you're gonna get your eye shot out by one of those BB guns!" Oh yeah, well this is man's stuff. How could any girl possibly know anything about war! But I didn't really say it even though I wanted to—I just thought it as I smiled at her.

Ah, those wonderful days of summer when you're a young boy and free from the cares of schoolwork and nuns armed with board pointers. Not every experience in the field involved our differences with the Polish. This was baseball season, and our personal playground provided all of the raw materials needed for that fun game. We would start by trampling the high grass down with the help of some of our other friends to create the infield, and then we'd hunt up some rocks or broken pieces of concrete for the bases. Since none of us could afford gloves, we used a large softball. Anytime that the ball would be lost in the high grass of the "outfield," a double would be allowed, but then even the batter would have to help search for the lost ball. Sometimes there would be the usual arguments about whether you were safe or out at first base or whatever, but the overriding emphasis was not on winning as much as it is today. Sure, there were times that we were kidded about being beat and how we would get even on the next day, but when the next day came, no one seemed to care or remember about yesterday. We were always looking ahead to the next day. But, now I find more enjoyment in the view from the rear view mirror—I appreciate the insight that comes from that perspective now. Looking back now I realize that those days in the field taught us so much more about life than just baseball. We felt that good feeling amongst friends that comes from doing something together—on our own. We learned the value of being self-starters, of being self-reliant, of teamwork and improvising—and so much more. Why heck, baseball was just the fun part of it.

Well now, we figured it'd be a safe time to return to "The Old Log" for fishing and swimming fun, and maybe Pencil Dillon would be gone now that the park swimming pool was open. We didn't care to go to the pool because there were too many rules we had to follow. That was really true for Fisty, and usually something would happen to get us kicked out, such as taunting the lifeguards. We knew that Caz Creek was dirty, but as DJ would say, "What the hell, with all the kids takin' a leak in the pool 'cause they're too lazy ta go to the bathroom—there isn't that much difference anyway!"

But, wouldn't ya' know it, there we were swimmin' in the creek and here comes Dillon again. "Vroom, Vroom!" But hold on, wait a minute, this time he doesn't say a single word. What the heck's goin' on? He calmly puts the kickstand down and gets off the motorcycle, pulls out a little notebook and starts readin', "Mullaney, you live on Sage Avenue, yer old man works on the railroad. Corrigan, you live on Sage Avenue too, yer old man's a scooper at the Concrete Grain elevators. Rossiter, yer easy, yer old man drives a bus on Seneca Street. I see him five or six times a day." You know what? Getting dressed is really difficult when you're shaking, and scared out of your wits.

"Jackie, this is gonna' hurt me a lot more than it will you!"

Dad was wrong again, but I sure wasn't about to tell him . . . and that was the last time we went swimmin' in Caz Creek.

-CHAPTER SEVEN-

DAD JOINS THE AIR CORPS

The adults were working most of the time, but every evening after dinner we would listen to the radio programs together—but only if our homework was finished first. From about seven o'clock to ten o'clock there were comedy and mystery shows on. We also played cards and other games. On the weekends we'd all go to Uncle Jim's house to play games while the adults talked at the kitchen table about the war, Jimmy McDonald and the three Rossiter boys. While they were talking they listened to music on the radio, and I remember hearing the voices of Bing Crosby, Al Jolson and Jo Stafford singing all about our boys serving "over there." Of course, if it were summertime all of us kids would be out playing Relieveio and Chase, or just sitting around and talking on someone's front porch. Sometimes it was so quiet on a summer evening that you could hear other people's conversation coming from a nearby porch. The adults were always talking about the war, about the boys serving in the military, and how long the war might go on. One night I could hear someone singing on a nearby radio. The usual static was crackling as Vera Lynne was singing, "The white cliffs of Dover." It had just gotten dark, and when the music stopped I realized that Dad was talking to Uncle Jim about how much he wanted to go into the military.

"Some of my friends at work told me that if I serve in the military, I'll get my citizenship real easy."

"Yeah Mike, but 'gol-durnit' that's a pretty dangerous way to go about it. Now you gotta remember about your family, and what would they do if somethin' happened to you."

"Yeah, You're right Jim, but the draft board gave me notice to be ready to be called into the army, and if they find out then about my citizenship problem then maybe I'd have more trouble than I already have now."

"No! Is that right, they may want to draft you at your age? How old are you now? Pushin' forty, aren't ya Mike?"

"Well no, not that old. I'm just thirty-six, but remember they're takin' every able-bodied man now, and I'm not one of those critical skill guys like an engineer or somethin'."

"Have you talked to Clara about this, Mike?"

"No, I only mentioned it once, but not this draft business." My dad suddenly spotted me on the neighbor's porch. "Who's that over there? Is that you, Mikey?"

"No, Dad, it's me, Jackie."

"Come on over here, son. Now Jackie, how much of that did you hear? Did you hear everything we were talkin' about?"

I felt scared as I said, "Yeah, Dad."

They both made me swear that I wouldn't tell anyone else at all, especially Mom. I swore that I would keep the secret until after he told everyone.

"But Jackie, when I make that decision I'll tell you first, okay?"

I said, "Sure, Dad," but I was really scared to think that I was the only one to know that my dad would probably be going off to the war soon. The summer fun continued on, but now I couldn't enjoy it as much because I was so worried about Dad leaving us someday. Dad told me that I would just have to "lock it out" and stop worrying because maybe the war would end and then he wouldn't have to go away. I knew that he was just saying that to keep me from worrying, so that made it even more difficult.

Money was always hard to come by so very few people could afford candy, and even food was scarce some of the time, so we learned how to satisfy both needs right in the neighborhood. Near the end of the summer we made "raids" on Mister Murphy's "Victory Garden" on the next street over. His property backed up to our famous field, so we'd sneak up to the garden by crawling on our stomach through the tall grass in the field. We'd pull the young tender carrots out of the ground, and eat them right away, but we'd first clean the carrots by spitting on them and then pulling them under the arm of our sweatshirt. The big red tomatoes were really good, too. We also spit on the mud that stuck to them, and then rubbed it off on our sweatshirt. Ah, but the very best food to raid were the dark purple cherries on the tree in old Mr. Scanlon's yard. The only problem was that Mr. Scanlon was retired and always on the lookout when the fruit was ripe. One day the three of us were up in the tree loading our mouths and pockets when he came out and yelled at us, "Hey, what are you kids doin' there?"

DJ and Fisty swore at him, probably out of fear, and I tried to jump over the fence to the next-door yard. My foot got caught in the top of the fence, causing me to go headfirst into a rock garden on the other side. My face was heading straight for the rocks, so I put my left arm up in front of myself to protect my head. I felt an awful pain in the arm, and I didn't remember much else because when I hit the rocks all the lights went out. A few minutes later I became aware that my sister Margaret was yelling at me while dragging me down the sidewalk between the houses towards home. When she saw the broken bone bulging up in my arm she got scared. She stopped and ran, yelling for help.

Doc Carden was away on vacation, so my arm had to be "set" by old Doc Shannahan, our cousin's doctor. A plaster cast was put on the arm, which meant that fun games like baseball were out for the rest of the summer, but there were certain benefits. I became quite a celebrity in the neighborhood because of the cast, and everybody wanted to sign their name and write a message on it.

DJ wrote, "How'd ya' like the cherries, Jackie?"

And Fisty, "Ye'r gonna have a hard time pickin' yer nose now!"

Well now, it turns out that old Doc Shannahan was practically blind—because when Doc Carden came back to his office and checked me out, he said, "Clara, the arm hasn't been set properly so we'll have to break it and set it again." Talk about knowin' how to scare a kid!

The next messages from my friends on the second cast were:

"How ya' doin', Jackie, hope they got it right this time!"

"Hey, it's a good thing ya' didn't break yer neck. Right, Jackie boy!"

One day, right after having the second cast put on my arm, I heard (Oh, oh!) old Mister Scanlon at our front door talking to my dad. I couldn't hear what they were saying, but I figured that I was gonna be in big trouble for climbin' in the cherry tree.

"Sure, Jackie's home Mister Scanlon. Come on in." I was so scared that I could hear my heart starting to pound. "Jackie, Mister Scanlon is here to see you. He has something for you."

I stood there frozen with fear, unable to say anything at all, ready for the worst.

"Jackie, here, this is for you. I'm sorry that you hurt your arm in my back yard. I've been worried about you ever since it happened." With that he handed me a basket of dark cherries from his tree! I couldn't believe it. He was saying that HE was sorry?

"Jackie, the next time you want some cherries from that tree you just come over and ask. You can have them anytime."

"You mean, ah, I mean, you're not mad at me, Mister Scanlon?"

"Jackie, you're the only one that didn't answer me with swear words, so no, I'm not mad at you. In fact, I felt real bad when I saw what happened to you, son."

"Thank you, Mister Scanlon, and I'm really sorry for climbing in your tree without permission. I won't do it again."

"Okay Jackie, and remember if you want some cherries just ring the bell and ask. Oh, and by the way, I hope you can get back to playing baseball again. I know your brother Mike is one heck of a catcher."

"Yeah, he sure is. Thanks for the cherries, Mister Scanlon."

Well, maybe baseball was out, but I could still go fishin' at "The Old Log." But no more messin' with "Pencil Dillon" now— not with a cast on my arm—and the memory of Dad's strap still fresh in my mind.

He sure was right about Mikey though, because Mikey was a really well-known ball player. Dad, Uncle Jim, Uncle Joe and I used to go to watch my brother play ball at Caz Park. That park had seen plenty of really good ball players including Warren Spahn, the famous left-handed pitcher who is now in the Hall of Fame. Mike was a catcher—quick as a cat. Nobody could steal second base (or any base) when he played. One fast motion: mask off, strong arm, "Yer out!" Dad would talk to important-looking men while we watched Mikey play; I heard those men ask a lot of questions about Mike's age and what grade he was in. They came every season to watch him play. Dad said they were professional baseball scouts looking for new talent to play when the war was over. One time I overheard a man talking to Dad.

"Mike, that boy of yours is a natural-born ball player; he has instincts that can't be taught. He reacts automatically as if he's seen it all before. Ya' know I've been scoutin' players for over forty years, and he just might be one of the finest prospects I've ever seen. Let's hope this damn war gets over soon, 'cause I'm anxious to see if my instincts are right about Mike. You can be real proud of him all right." Dad looked over at me, and realized that I heard what the man had said.

"Well now, I'm proud of all of our children. Say, have you met Jackie, Mike's younger brother?"

"Hello, Jackie, are you a ball player too?"

"Oh, yeah I play baseball, but not like Mikey—he's really good."

Dad said, "Jackie's a natural-born fisherman. You should see the size of some of the Black Bass he's caught right over there in Caz Creek." He pointed in the direction of the creek.

"Hey, no kiddin', right over there in the park? Ya' know Jackie, I love to go fishin', so the next time I'm in town what say you take me over to your favorite spot, okay?"

I could tell the man was just trying to be nice, but he didn't really mean it. Kids can always tell when a grown up doesn't mean it. We all wondered why they were that way. I nodded and said "sure" anyway. Mike was just fourteen at the time, so the baseball scouts would come back every summer to watch him play. Pretty soon everyone in South Buffalo knew about him, and I was pretty excited about the whole thing.

"Hey Jackie, I bet yer brother's gonna be a big-time ball player someday, right?"

"Well, I don't know, DJ, besides he's only fourteen, and that's not old enough for the big leagues."

"Boy, I wish I could be a big-time hero like that someday.'

"Maybe someday you will be, DJ. Hey, who knows, maybe we'll all be famous someday."

Fisty said, "I wanna be rich someday and be able to buy plenty a' shoes and stuff like that, so's I don't have to wear my brother's hand-me-down clothes. That way I could have extra shoes without holes in the soles for when it rains." We all agreed that having shoes without holes would be pretty neat all right.

The days of late summer seemed to hurry by, as they usually do when back to school time was coming closer. Everyday there was a steady stream of news about the war on the radio, and every Saturday afternoon in the "Movietone News" at the Orpheum. We heard about places with strange-sounding names, especially in the Pacific war. That year brought steady news about The Solomon Islands, and that was a constant reminder of Joe being a prisoner somewhere. Whenever the Solomons were mentioned, we would always hear the adults talking about Joe. One day we heard the adults talking about places called Sicily and Italy, and how Joe's brothers, Tom and Phil, and Jim McDonald were involved in heavy fighting there. Since they were now off fighting in the war we had stopped calling them Jimmy, Joey, Tommy and Philsie. A young boy's name just didn't sound right now that they were soldiers— in danger—and so far away from home. With the news about Italy, we began to worry a lot more about our cousins, and that worry could be most easily seen on the faces of Uncle Jim, Aunt Mary, and Uncle Joe. By looking at the big world map with Aunt Mary, I was learning all about the geography of the world, but I would rather have learned about those places in school—not that way. Fisty and DJ were always asking about my cousins, especially about Joe.

"Do those dirty little Japs beat him up? I hear they torture our guys when they capture 'em, Jackie."

We had all heard rumors that the American prisoners were being abused. My nightmares were more than enough, so I didn't want to think about it.

"I don't know, Fisty, but I just don't wanna talk about it, okay?"

"Well, those dirty little Nips better look out 'cause my brother Gerry just joined up."

Both DJ and I were surprised because Gerry was only seventeen. DJ had a quizzical look as he asked, "What branch, Fisty?"

"What are you, kiddin' me? Marines a' course, just like Joe."

"When does he have to leave, Fisty?"

"Next week Monday, Jackie."

For just an instant I caught a quick glimpse of fear in Fisty's eyes as he answered my question, but he covered it up right away.

"But don't worry about Gerry. He can take care a' himself all right!"

We were always afraid, but we followed the example of the adults: We tried not to let it show, but that wasn't very easy at our age. When school started in September we noticed that more and more fathers had gone away to the war. When Sister Mary would say to one of the boys, "You'll have to bring your father in about this." Oftentimes the answer would be:

"I can't, Sister."

"Why not?"

"'Cause he's gone away to the war."

Soon, even Sister Mary stopped asking to see our fathers. And before long our dad would also be going off to fight in the war.

The kitchen table was always the place where we had our meals and casual family talks, but it was also the place where important family decisions were made. When Dad called everybody into the kitchen after dinner to sit down, we all knew that something important was about to happen. When he announced that he had enlisted in the Army Air Corps, Mom let out a gasp, and the rest of us went into what we called "scared quiet." I was so overcome with fear that I had completely forgotten that he had broken his promise not to tell anyone else before telling me.

"Oh my God, Mike! Why would you want to do that, especially with all the worry down the street at the Rossiter's and McDonald's?"

"Clara, I had no choice. It was either join the Air Corps or be drafted into the army."

"They were going to draft you—with five kids and all? You're not lying to us now, are you Mike?"

"Have you ever known me to tell a lie, Clara?"

"Well no, Mike, it's just that . . ." Her voice had a mixture of apprehension, fear, and yet a tone of resignation. The Irish are well conditioned to adapting and overcoming the many problems in life—once they know deep down that a problem is unchangeable. That ability came directly from our history as a people—along with hundreds of years of frustration.

"I guess I suspected this all along, Mike. But now what are we going to do, trying to live on a small military pay? How are we ever gonna survive?" She was already trying to figure out a way to deal with this new situation.

"Well, there'll be dependent allowances, and maybe the older kids could work some odd jobs to help out."

Mikey, Margaret and Maureen all said together, "We can do it, Mom!"

Mary was so afraid that she just stared straight ahead, while I said, "I can help some, too!" Dad smiled at me.

"Sure ya' can, Jackie. Maybe you can run errands for the people on the street." His saying that made me feel really important.

Mom said, "Come over here Mary, and sit on my lap." She had some comforting words for Mary that seemed to calm her fears.

Dad continued, "I've already talked to the relatives about this, and they said they'd all help out. In fact, Jim says that he's gonna switch to the four-to-twelve shift at the railroad; that way he'll be available during the mornings and afternoons if he's needed. Joe says he'll take over the watch when he comes home at five thirty until bedtime. The way they all offered to help out it made me feel a lot better about this whole thing."

"But Mike, you haven't said when you have to leave."

"My train leaves for San Antonio, Texas in ten days. I'll have my uniform in just a few days."

When I saw my dad for the first time in that khaki uniform, I sensed that our world was changing rapidly. I just knew that our life would never be the same again. We were all at the train station when he left, and every one of us had a feeling of loneliness that day. Several years after his announcement that day at the kitchen table we found out that Dad had told his first lie to us. He wanted so much to get his citizenship and to join up with the military to fight that he was willing to lie to us for the first time ever. Then again, he did say, "Did you ever know me to tell a lie?"

-CHAPTER EIGHT-

THE GAMBLER

By now my arm had healed and that itchy cast was finally taken off, so I spent all my free time looking for odd jobs to help out with the money at home. I also wrote my first letter to Dad, and we put all of our letters into one big envelope to mail to Texas. That first letter was pretty clumsy because writing letters was something new to me, and he hadn't been away from home very long. My letter-writing skills would improve with time—but I would miss him more and more with the passing of that time.

Like my older sisters and brother, I was doing odd jobs for money to help out at home, so I hadn't seen very much of DJ and Fisty lately—except at school. One Saturday afternoon, after I finished running some errands and cutting grass, I decided to go fishing in Caz Park. I went alone, and this time I decided to try my luck at the stone bridge, not far from "The Old Log." After fishing for an hour or so, I heard voices of people using strange expressions. Later on I learned that it was something called a crap game on the bridge above. I had never heard such strange words before, and my curiosity caused me to pack up my gear and see what was going on. As I stood there watching for a few minutes an elderly Italian man dressed in construction clothes said to me,

"Well, you gonna shoot?"

He spoke with a heavy accent and I didn't understand him, so he repeated the question. By then I had seen some other people "shoot," so I sort of knew what to do. I picked up the dice to shoot, not knowing exactly what I was supposed to do, and he said,

"Whoa, where's da money? When you pick'a the dice up you gotta put down da money!"

I had only one dollar in my pocket from two days of doing odd jobs, but I didn't want to lose it. I was confused, and at that moment since I had already picked up the dice, I thought I was obligated to put my money down. I was scared as I placed my only dollar down on the cement, all the while thinking that I was going to lose the reward of my hard labors. I rolled the dice as I had seen the others do, and then just stood there as he said, "You win!"

He began to instruct me on what to do while he made what he called "side bets." "Let it ride, you hot! Ten bucks he makes little Joe. Ten bucks he makes that fever. I'm covered. You covered! Go ahead. Shoot again. Shoot again!"

My head was spinning, and boy was I ever scared and nervous. I had never before seen so much money! The old man then said, "Drag some." He had to explain the meaning of that expression to me. After a few more minutes he said, "Okay, you crapped out." He then took me aside and said I made him, "Lots'a money." He told me that I should stuff all that money down in my pockets because the bills were all hanging out. His advice to me was:

"Go home now, boy. Stuff that money down in "you" pockets and run like hell, 'cause maybe somebody wants ta take all 'dat' money away from you!"

I took his advice and "ran like hell" all the way home. On the way home, my imagination told me that there was somebody hiding behind every tree and bush just waiting to pounce on me for this huge bundle of cash. I didn't stop running until I had covered the mile or so to our house. I fumbled nervously with the skeleton key to unlock the door. I was out of breath and panting as I pulled the money out of my pockets and piled it onto the kitchen table. I was so thankful that nobody was home. My hands were trembling as I began to unfold the bills and count them. Oh, My God. Two hundred and forty seven dollars! What should I do? Hide the money! But, where? I know—in the rafters down in the spooky cellar. That's it! I wrapped the money in a brown paper bag and stuffed it up into the rafters in a corner of the wall where there was a pocket area. During the next few days my imagination hounded me. What if Mom found out? What would I say? What if the police found out? Would I go to jail? Would Dad give me a lickin' when he came home from the Air Corps? My emotions moved from fear to elation and guilt, then back to fear again. Mom began to ask questions.

"What's wrong with you, Jackie? Don't you feel well?" I was so scared and upset that I couldn't stand it anymore. I decided that I just had to tell her what happened.

"*What did you say? How much, Jackie?* Jesus, Mary and Joseph, two hundred and forty seven dollars! Oh, my God!"

I thought that she was gonna really punish me, but after a time she calmed down and became convinced that my story was true, that I hadn't stolen the money. She said she would put the money in the bank for emergencies. Now back in those days an emergency in our family meant getting a new pair of shoes two weeks after the old pair had a large hole in the sole. I figured that the money would be consumed by one emergency after another.

She said that I was "not to tell anyone about this money—ever!" She had me convinced, and besides I already figured that I was gonna go to jail if anyone ever found out.

"Jackie, you also have to swear to God that you'll NEVER again get involved in gambling." Since the memory of that whole episode was so nerve racking for me, that promise was easy to keep.

For a long time afterwards whenever we would get any small thing extra in the family, I was always under the impression that our "windfall" was the source of the money needed. Eventually, I completely forgot about that stressful day—until many years later. I was eighteen at the time and I'd been saving my money to buy a used car. I was getting discouraged because it was taking such a long time to save enough money when Mom handed me an old brown paper bag. In the bag was a savings account passbook that had been opened in nineteen forty-three, the first entry was two hundred and forty seven dollars; with interest it now totaled three hundred and thirty eight dollars. She said that the old brown bag was the very same bag that I had used to hide the cash in the basement. I was shocked to think how she had resisted using that money through all of those many years of hardship, and now I was at a complete loss to find the words to describe how I felt because of what she had done for me . . .

Fall was here: Morning sunlight was at a lower angle each day, causing long shadows on the wet grass. The colors on the trees were bright; the colors of the fallen leaves were more muted. The leaves on the ground that we played in had an unforgettable pungent odor that seemed to fit right in with the season. People on the street would rake their leaves into a big pile near the curb before burning them. The smoke drifted slowly up into the trees above, filling the brisk October air with an unforgettable scent. It was a pleasant odor, reminding me of the "Sugar Barrel" pipe tobacco burning in Uncle Joe's pipe. The morning frost was already causing us to think about winter: snowball fights, and building snow "forts"; King of the Castle on the large piles of snow on Seneca Street; and ice hockey on the pond in Caz Park.

But for now, we were still playing baseball in the field, and "pick-up" football in Caz Park. I was a running back, which I hated because when you were tackled all of the kids wanted to "pile on." Sometimes I thought I was gonna die because I could hardly breathe. Mikey gave me some of his old football equipment for protection, including a pair of official style pants. The pants had elastic pads at the knees, and insert pads in the hips and legs area. They were a dark tan color—and I can still remember exactly what they looked like after all these years. I was so proud.

At that time of year we always looked forward to Johnny coming home on break from the seminary because it meant playing touch football in the street. Johnny didn't only teach the ins and outs of the game—he taught us values to live by. I can still see and hear him now, with his blond hair and smiling dark brown eyes, as he'd say with a warm smile and a soft voice, "Okay Jackie, now it's your turn. Go down past O'Donnell's house, and then cut left just past the fire hydrant. I'll throw you the ball as you're making your break back towards the middle of the street."

I felt important being given all of those instructions and

responsibility. If you caught the ball he would cheer the loudest, but more importantly he would never say anything to make you feel bad if you didn't catch the ball. In fact, he would tell you quietly what you needed to do to catch the ball the next time.

"Never get discouraged and quit, guys. Always remember that giving up will only guarantee that you'll miss out on an awful lot of fun in life." We'd play for hours in the brisk air before taking an apple pie and milk break in Aunt Mary's pantry.

It seems that all fun things in life come and go so quickly, so before we knew it Johnny was on his way back to the seminary again. Before leaving though, he would always come down to our house to talk to my mom at the kitchen table about his decision to become a priest. He'd confide in her that he was still uncertain about wanting to take his "final vows," and that he felt the pressure of the high expectations because of his intention to become a priest. In those days, if a young man decided to become a priest it was considered an extremely high honor—both in the family, and in the neighborhood. Respect for the religious people was at a very high ebb back then. I didn't fully understand all of those more complicated adult problems at that time, and only as I look back now from the future do I realize the important issues that I had witnessed. I realize now that being a witness was an honor and a privilege . . .

During that time of year I began to notice that our differences of opinion with the Polish boys seemed to be at least temporarily forgotten. I began to think that they might also be occupied with the same fun sports as us. Hmm . . . well, maybe we're not so different after all.

It had now been three months since Dad left for Texas, and we were beginning to miss him more each day—especially when we'd see a bus go by on Seneca Street. When he was home he used to blow the horn and wave every time we saw him passing by, and now that image was becoming just a fading memory. We got word one day that he was on his way to Illinois for further training before being assigned to a permanent duty station. He said that when his training was finished, he'd be home for ten days in

December before shipping out overseas. We counted the days on the calendar until December the tenth, the day when he'd be coming home. That's when we realized that he would be gone by the twentieth—just five days before Christmas. The realization that he wouldn't be home for Christmas had all of us depressed, but then Mom came up with a great idea. She said we could simply move our family Christmas up to the seventeenth and celebrate early. There! That's settled, now we could all look forward to that time with Dad without something else to worry about. Mom always seemed to know what to do.

I decided that I was going to work extra hard to buy Dad a very special present for Christmas. Well, I worked really hard but the cost of what I wanted was so high that I knew that I could never save enough money to buy the present I had in mind. I told my brother and sisters about what I had hoped to buy, and they all thought it was a real good idea. We talked it over and decided to pool all our money together to try to buy that special present. We made just barely enough money, but not until only two days before our own family "Christmas."

"A gold Hamilton pocket watch! Oh my God, kids, how did you ever manage to afford something so beautiful?"

We all said, "Look on the back of the watch, Dad!"

He read the inscription out loud. "We'll all be with you all of the time, Dad. Margaret, Mike, Maureen, Jackie and Mary. 12/17/43."

Mom was shocked with surprise and tears because we were able to keep our secret to ourselves.

Maureen said, "It was Jackie's idea, but he couldn't afford it so we decided to pool all our money together."

I said, "The words on the back were Margaret's idea."

Dad took a long time to say something, and he just stared at the watch in his hands while fumbling with the gold chain and silently reading the words on the back cover. He kept his head down as he spoke quietly. "I—I just don't know what to say, kids. I'm gonna be thinking of all of you whenever I look at this to tell the time. I never thought I'd own something as beautiful as this—

ever." His voice was breaking, so he stopped talking and gave all of us a big hug.

Only now, so many years later do I fully appreciate what the four of us "older" kids accomplished in our joint effort back then. Mike and I cleaned out garages, cut grass, cleaned yards, ran errands, shoveled snow and searched the entire neighborhood for pop and beer bottles to return to the stores for the deposit. Margaret and Maureen did baby-sitting, dog sitting and grooming, as well as running errands. We were able to save one hundred and twenty dollars in only three months' time. Our pay probably averaged about five cents per hour, and we gave up all candy and movies to save that money. None of us could remember what gifts we received that day, but many years later we all agreed that December seventeen, nineteen forty-three was the all-time best Christmas we ever had.

-CHAPTER NINE-

DAD GOES AWAY TO THE WAR

The time for Dad to leave came so quickly, and it was made even more difficult because there was still no word about Joe. When I watched Aunt Mary hug my Dad extra long and extra tight that day, I realized that she was also hugging and thinking about her sons, especially Joe. Everyone from the three families came to see Dad off at the train station, and we knew that this time he would be much farther away, and now he would be in danger. After he went away the bad dreams got worse, and came more often. As Dad said goodbye to me, he told me to help Mike take care of the coal furnace, and whispered "You're the men of the house now." As I watched the end of the train disappear down the tracks, I felt my uncle Jim's arm around my shoulder.

"Jackie, it's a tough business, this world of ours, especially at your age. In case you're thinkin' that maybe your dad won't come back safe, never mind thinkin' that way. He'll be back, and we'll all be prayin' for him in the meantime, right?" I nodded yes.

"Now I want to tell ya somethin' I learned a long time ago. Did ya ever notice how good ya felt after a few rainy days when the sun came out again? I don't mean just good, but really good. Well, that's how it is in life: We appreciate a sunny day so much more only if we've known some rainy days. You might not understand what I'm sayin' now, but I want ya ta be always lookin' ahead to the sunny days, Jackie. You have to believe that the good days will come back again, son.

And Jackie, your dad and I talked things over many times, and he asked me to be here for you if you ever need someone to talk to;

that's why I'm workin' the late shift now. If you ever want to stop by our house anytime, just walk right in and I'll be glad to see ya', okay?" I nodded again. "In fact, even if you just want ta stop in for no reason at all son, well that's okay too. I'll be glad to see ya' anytime. Is that a deal?"

"Okay, Uncle Jim."

"Then let's shake on it, Jackie."

From that day on a new relationship started for me with my uncle Jim, as he became a second father to me, well not really, but maybe more like the grandfather I had never known. We would check all the news about the war together, and then one day he confided something to me about my dad that I hadn't known.

"Jackie, your dad and I talked this over before he went away, and he told me to use my best judgment to make sure that you could handle this information. Ya' see, we want ya' to know that he's a machine gunner in a B17 bomber, flyin' out of England. I'm not sure, but I think the base is called Alconbury. Now he didn't want to tell you in that first letter that you got 'cause he wanted to leave it up to me to see if you could handle that kind of information, and I think ya' can. What do ya' think? Was I right?" I nodded yes and said,

"Yeah, Uncle Jim, it's okay. Is that a dangerous job?"

"Well, Jackie, in wartime there aren't many safe jobs, believe me I know. Ya' know Jackie, I told ya' I'd never lie to ya', didn't I?" I trusted this wise old man, and he always seemed to know what I was thinking just by looking into my eyes so I didn't even have to answer.

"By the way Jackie, why not pull that letter out right now and we'll read it together again." He smiled when I showed surprise that he knew I carried it with me in my pocket all the time.

"Okay, Uncle Jim."

> Dear Mike and Jackie,
>
> How ya doin', boys? Well what do you know, here I am a crewmember on a B17 bomber—can you imagine that! I'm still learning and practicing with experienced crewmembers, and there's a lot more to learn so I haven't

been on an actual mission yet. I hope it'll be soon though, 'cause I'm pretty anxious to get started with the real McCoy. I just had to write this letter after I checked the time on my beautiful new watch. I still can't believe I own such a famous timepiece. I'll never forget that day, boys. By the way, I'm writing a separate letter of thanks to the girls.

Boys, while flying over here I had quite an experience when our flight plan took us right over Ireland, a place that I had seen only in my dreams for so many years. The sight of that beautiful green island caused me to think of our ancestors, and all the heartache they suffered at the hands of the British. How strange, I thought, that so many other Irish-Americans like myself are now on the way to help the country that treated our families so badly. But then I remembered what my dad used to say, "Everything in life comes full circle, and then returns to the beginning." Our beginnings, our heritage, and our hearts will always be with that land of our ancestors, but now a much bigger evil is loose in the world, one that threatens all people as once our own were threatened. It's time now to put aside our bad memories of the past, even if only temporarily, and pull together now for the common good.

We have to remember that we're all Americans first now, and to do whatever our country needs done. It's a great country that has given all of us the freedom and opportunity that we had hoped for. Make no mistake; there will always be that part of our hearts and minds where we hold the memory of who we are and where we came from. We'll keep our dear heritage of the past, but for now we need to put all of our energy into helping bring peace back to the world again.

I'll write to you both every time I get a chance. I want you to take good care of Mom and the girls for me, boys. I know I can depend on you boys. And that's no malarkey!

P.S. I'll always be in your corner, so keep your chin up!

Love, Dad

I began to see more of Fisty and DJ over the Christmas break, and I was glad to get back to snowball fights and snow forts. The guys were now asking a lot more questions about Dad.

"So yer dad's a machine gunner now, huh Jackie? Bet that's a lot different than drivin' a bus, huh!"

"Yeah Fisty, I guess it's different, but it scares me 'cause I've seen pictures of those guys in the newsreels at the Orpheum. I just hope nothin' happens to him, ya' know what I mean?"

DJ said, "I'm glad my old man don't have to go over there and fight those Nazis and Nips."

Fisty was always the one most sure of himself when he spoke: "Aw, stop worryin', you guys, nothin's gonna happen; those guys wear special protection. I saw it in the 'GI Joe' comic books at the candy store."

"Hey Fisty, how's yer brother Gerry doin' in the Marines these days?"

"Au, he's doin' okay, Jackie. He's out some place in California gettin' ready to go kick hell out a' those dirty little Japs. He wrote me a letter about how it is in the Marines. He says they're tough guys, but that's the way he likes it. He says he's gonna get even fer Joe."

I said, "I wish we'd hear somethin' about Joe. It sure has been a long time now . . . Boy, I hope he's okay." We were always worried because the war seemed to go on forever. We needed something to take our minds off it.

I said, "Hey, whaddya say, let's go hitchin' cars after supper when it gets dark."

"Wow, great idea!"

"Okay, see ya tonight down at the corner."

Now hitching cars is one of the most dangerous things we ever did back then, and if our parents had found out they would have had a heart attack. The trick is to hide near a corner where there's a stop sign. When a car comes to a stop on the icy street, you sneak out from behind cover and grab onto the car's rear bumper. Then as the car starts accelerating you go down into a crouch and ski in your boots behind the car. What you have to watch out for is a dry spot on the road, or the worst thing—a high manhole cover. I didn't see the manhole cover—then WHAM!

"Jackie, Jackie! Are you all right?"

"Oh, I don't know, everything hurts, especially my back."

"Come on, we better get you home right away!"

Mom was in a state of shock. "Oh my God, Jackie, what in God's name were you hitching cars for? Where does it hurt? Come on; let's get you down to Doc Carden right away. Jesus, Mary and Joseph!"

After a couple days of tests, Doc Carden told Mom that he wanted her to take me to Children's Hospital—but not for any injury from the accident. He said that was just bruises, but he was concerned about my kidneys.

"Doc, that one scares me now, 'cause that problem's been with the Rossiters for years. In fact, Mike's brother Jack is the one Jackie is named after. Jack died from this same problem when he was only twenty-eight."

"Yes Clara, I know about it, and that's why we want to run some extra tests. You see, Joe told me about the family history when I first saw Johnny for the same problem several years ago."

"Doc, do you think everything's gonna be . . . "

"Now Clara, let's not get ahead of ourselves and jump to conclusions here. You take him to see this specialist here at Children's Hospital—he's a good man with this sort of thing. And remember, this one we caught real early—and that makes a very big difference."

During the walk home I was scared and asked a lot of questions.

"Mom, what does that big word, Nephrology, mean?"

She answered all my questions. She said it was because she wanted me to know everything that she knew. "I'll always tell you exactly what they tell me, Jackie. I don't want you to imagine anything that's not true. That would be the worst thing that I could do, to have you believing something from your imagination that's not true."

Mom was always honest with me that way. She treated me like a grown-up, and because of that I always trusted her. Before my first visit to the hospital I already knew what my illness was, and how it had been in the family for many years. I was also told that treatment would work better because it was discovered in the early stages. Of course, no matter how much I knew about it I was still scared, but I would never admit it. I wanted to be tough just like the adults.

Johnny was "ordained" at Saint Bridget's Church in January of nineteen forty-four. Normally an altar boy isn't allowed to take part in the ceremony, but an exception was made this time for Mikey. An Ordination Mass is a very solemn ceremony presided over by the Bishop, and includes many other priests on the altar acting as deacons. The church was overflowing with everyone from our neighborhood, as well as some people we didn't even know. I saw a lot of military uniforms in the congregation—friends of all of our families who were home on leave. Monsignor Foley was on the altar taking part in the ceremony, and he was as happy as though Johnny was his own son. Actually, Johnny was being ordained early because there was a shortage of priests due to the war. Now that shortage news had started Aunt Mary and Uncle Joe to worry about something new: the possibility that Johnny, the last of the boys at home, would also have to serve in the military as a chaplain. But then came the death of the famous five Sullivan boys who were all killed at once. After that, the government made it a policy not to have so many boys from the same family exposed to imminent danger in order to prevent another family tragedy. It was some comfort to them when the new policy was announced in November, nineteen forty-three. Of course, it was also a mixed blessing because the death of those five Irish boys was a reminder to all of us that so many boys in one family could be wiped out in the blink of an eye.

There was a party that evening at the school hall, and for the time being at least Uncle Joe and Aunt Mary were able to enjoy the evening. They were really proud of their son becoming a priest. Before dinner there were prayers and silence for all of our relatives in the military, and that started me thinking about Dad. Five of our relatives had now gone away to the war. Counting Fisty's brother,

Gerry, there were six close friends and relatives who were now in the military. Someone said there were over twenty-five people in all from our street now serving in the military. I guess we all knew that the number was high because Father Johnny was one of the few men of draft age still at home. He was assigned temporarily to Saint Bridget's until a permanent assignment would take place. This made everyone really happy because now we could go to Mass and see both Johnny and Mike on the altar. Ever since Dad went away, we called my brother "Mike," instead of Mikey because he was the oldest "man" in the house now. It sure seemed strange to see Johnny in the clothes of a priest. Fisty and DJ came to the party, and even Fisty was on his best behavior when he saw Johnny dressed as a priest for the first time.

"Wow, Jackie, he sure does look different now. I wonder if he'll ever play football in the street with us anymore?"

"Well, let's just ask him, guys." Before I could ask about football, Father Johnny said, "Fisty, where did you get those bruises on your neck and face?"

"Oh, it's nothin', Father, I got into a little scrap with a guy on the next street over." Fisty looked away nervously as he answered, but it didn't register with me right away.

I said, "Father Johnny, can you still play football, I mean since you're a priest and all now?"

"Why sure, Jackie! This collar can come off to play football again. In fact, it's nice and warm out now, so how's about tomorrow mornin', guys?"

"Father Johnny, do we have to call ya' 'Father' when we play football now?"

"I'll tell you what, Patrick: You call me 'Johnny', and I'll call you "Fisty." Now how does that sound to you?" Johnny smiled at Fisty.

Fisty got the meaning right away. "Father Johnny, yer okay!"

"Yer not so bad yourself, Fisty! By the way, how's your brother Gerry doin', and how's your mom and dad holdin' up these days?"

"Oh, Mom's all right, and Gerry's gettin' ready to ship out soon."

"And how 'bout your dad?"

Fisty lowered his eyes. "Oh, he's okay I guess."

Johnny knew something; I saw it in his eyes.

"I'll say a prayer for him, as well as your mom and brother, Fisty."

"Okay guys, see ya' all in the mornin', about nine o'clock, okay?"

Okay, Father Johnny!"

Fisty was right; it did seem strange to be calling him "Father" now.

DJ said, "Well, it seems funny to call him "Father," but he doesn't act any different now. I mean, he doesn't act like the other adults who say things that they don't really mean." DJ said exactly what we had all been thinking about Johnny, and that's just one of the reasons why we liked being around him. Come to think of it, that's really why we liked Johnny so much. He was still a kid at heart—so much like us in so many ways. He made us feel good because he treated us as equals.

Johnny took me aside after the party to talk to me about my kidney problem. He told me that he had the same problem now for several years, and that it wasn't any big deal. He said he had to take some medicine everyday, and had to go in for tests every six months. "You know, Jackie, they say that in many cases it can just suddenly go away as fast as it came—that's called "remission." You see, we're very lucky, well actually blessed because they caught it early for us, and nowadays they know a lot more about how to treat it. So Jackie, don't let it worry you, and if you ever want to talk about it just tell my mom and she'll get in touch with me, okay?"

"Okay, Father Johnny. See ya' in the mornin'!"

A few days after the football game in the street, Johnny paid a visit to Fisty's house while we were in school. He had quite a talk with Tom Mullaney, Fisty's father. "Tom, I'm not here to discuss IF you've been hitting Patrick, but WHY you've been hitting him."

"What's that ya say? Now who's been fillin' yer head with those lies, Johnny Rossiter? That's absolutely not true what yer sayin'!"

"Never mind that now Tom. You see I've been doin' some checking in various places, and I'm convinced that you've been abusing Patrick. I'm here to tell you that I will not sit idly by while that's going on!"

"Priest, are you threatenin' me, right here in my own home?"

"You can look on my words any way that you wish, Tom Mullaney. And now don't be lookin' so menacingly at me because you don't scare me one bit. I'm not some young boy that you can intimidate, you know!"

Mrs. Mullaney gasped when Mister Mullaney said, *"You get the hell out a' my home right now, Priest!"*

"Now, don't worry Margaret, that sort a' thing doesn't bother me. Tom, just so there's no misunderstanding I'll tell you before I go just what I'm gonna do: I'm going first to the railroad to speak with the general superintendent about this, and then I'm goin' back down to Murphy's Bar and Grill where you spend so much of your time."

"Now what in the hell would you be goin' to Murphy's for?"

"Because the Murphy family doesn't like people who abuse children, and from what I was able to learn from the patrons, none of those men have any tolerance for that sort a' thing, either. So, do you get my meanin' here, Tom? *Do you REALLY get my meanin'?"*

Tom Mullaney became silent as Johnny said goodbye to Margaret. "Take care of yourself, Margaret, and remember we're just down the street if you need us for anything—anything at all now, Margaret." He turned his attention back to Mister Mullaney.

"Tom, now there'll be people nearby who will be listening for anything at all, so I'd best not hear about any more problems here, or you're gonna have a lot more trouble than your job or your hangout. Make no mistake about that, not ONCE more, Tom! Oh, and by the way, I've also been in touch with your son, Gerry, out in California. He says to tell you that you'll have to deal with him if there's any more of this sort of thing. Goodbye for now, Tom."

After Father Johnny's visit that day, it marked the end of the problems at the Mullaney home. Fisty seemed like a new person after that: less tense, much more relaxed and happy from that day on. We could only guess what he had been going through because we'd never bring it up with him.

A letter from DAD!

Dear Jackie,

I'm writing this letter to just you this time because I heard about the kidney problem that Doc Carden found. Mom tells me that it's under control, and Doc says that you're going to be okay. Thank God, Son. I know that Mom has been very honest with you, and I agree with that way, Jackie. You know that the problem runs in the Rossiter family, so I'm glad that it was discovered early and can be controlled.

I'm gonna keep in touch with you and Mom on this one, so you can expect to see plenty of letters from me, okay? Also, I sent a letter of congratulations to Father Johnny, and I asked him to talk to you from time to time—if that's okay with you. I feel kind of helpless being here, almost three thousand miles away, but my prayers will be with you everyday, Jackie. God bless you, Son. Write me a letter soon.

Love, Dad

Dear Dad,

I was really happy to get your letter today. I'm feeling real good now. Mom and the doctors told me everything, and Johnny talked to me too. Johnny says its not any big deal, and that it just might go away someday. I have to take two pills everyday and drink lots of water. Mom takes me to the hospital once a week now, but they said pretty soon maybe once a month will be enough.

Uncle Jim says you're a machine gunner in a big bomber airplane now. That must be dangerous, huh? Write me a letter soon and tell me what it's like being in a big bomber like that, okay? I spend a lot of time with Uncle Jim now, and I like him a lot.

Johnny's Ordination Mass was really somethin', with

lots of priests on the altar, and the Bishop was even there.
They let Mike come on the altar too. Johnny's at home a lot
now, so we play football in the street if it doesn't snow.
When the snow comes my buddies and me build a fort and
put plenty of snowballs inside.

Fisty and DJ are always askin' me about your job in the
Air Corps. They said to say hello. I saw a model airplane kit
for the B-17 bomber, and I'm savin' up to buy it. I miss you,
Dad. Write soon, and tell me all about the war, okay?

Love, Jackie

P.S. Don't worry about the girls, Dad. Mike and me are
lookin' out for the girls and Mom, so don't you be worryin'
now.

-CHAPTER TEN-

EVERYDAY LIFE IN THE NEIGHBORHOOD

On Saturday mornings during the winter, Fisty, DJ and I would go around looking for snow-shoveling jobs to earn some extra money. We could usually earn a total of two or three dollars by working six hours together. We each took our share home to our moms to help out with the family expenses. Mike did the same jobs with his friends. If we made a little extra money, we stopped on the way home at Jimmy The Greek restaurant on Seneca Street to get a "Texas red hot" and a glass of chocolate milk. Shoveling snow was a common practice for most of the boys in South Buffalo. Besides shoveling snow during the winter, we were responsible for shoveling coal into the cellar for the furnace. After the coal was burned, we hauled the ashes out to the curb for weekly pickup. We hated to see rain or wet snow because we knew that when the ashes were wet, the can was going to be really heavy. In those days we were always taught that it was sinful to waste anything, including ashes. Besides, there was always some smart person around who would figure out a use for just about everything, so we used the ashes for traction on the slippery sidewalk ice, or we put them under the wheel of a car that was stuck in the snow. We would also push on the back of a car that was stuck to help free it from an ice rut, even if we didn't know the driver. It was always customary to help someone in trouble, and that person would help you in return if you had a problem. That practice was known as "being neighborly."

Shoveling coal into the furnace was a job I shared with Mike. Dad had taught us how to load the coal into the firebox, and then

"bank" the fire to make it last through the night. Banking the fire
meant that after the coal was burning sufficiently, you reduced the
amount of air going into the firebox by partially closing the air
intake damper control. Mike and I would share the job, and would
take turns getting up at five in the morning to load more coal,
shake the grates to get rid of the ashes, and then bank the fire
again for the start of the day. Right after school that same routine
had to be repeated again. If you were late just once, the fire would
go out, which meant that the house would be cold and the water
pipes could possibly freeze and break. There wasn't any insulation
in the walls, so the pipes were exposed on the inside of the walls,
using the heat inside the house to keep them from freezing.
Sometimes we'd use the pipes as a message system by banging on
them with a butter knife to complain about noise coming from
the upstairs flat, or use it as a "secret" message code. There wasn't
an automatic pilot on the hot water heater, so we had to light it
with a big wooden "blue tip" match before we could take a bath. If
you forgot to turn it off after your bath, the pipes would start
banging, and we'd catch hell from Dad.

The coal company would deliver a ton of "anthracite" coal to
our house about once a month, but we didn't have a driveway so
the coal was dumped out in the street in front of the house. From
there we had to load it into a wheelbarrow we borrowed from
Mister Corrigan, and then dump it into the coal bin through the
cellar window. It usually took about fifty or sixty trips with the
wheelbarrow. Mike and I would share the job, and we were always
tired when the job was finished. Just keeping the house warm in
those days was a big job, and all of the other neighborhood boys
had to do the same chore as we did.

Boy, how I hated to go into that spooky cellar at night. I
imagined that every shadow on the walls was an evil monster just
waiting to cut my throat or strangle my skinny little neck. Each
creak of the floors above and every squeak from the furnace meant
something sinister in my mind. But the scariest part of my job at
night was when I had to go into the coal bin, a separate room in
the corner where the coal was stored. There wasn't any light to

turn on, so it was always as black as the coal in there! There were shadows on the walls coming from the dull light of a forty-watt bulb about twenty feet away. My imagination told me each time that there was an ugly monster hiding just behind the partition in the dark. That imagined vicious killer of little boys was just waiting for me to stick my head inside that dark room where he was lurking. My heart would beat faster and faster, the adrenaline would begin to pump rapidly into my blood, causing sweat to build up on my skin in spite of the cold winter . . . and then . . . nothing! *Nothing else would happen. That was it. No evil monster, nothing. I was always physically and mentally exhausted afterwards, and I'd reason with myself that the worry was all very silly. But, on the very next night my fears would start up all over again. The hard work wasn't the only reason that I was always happy when winter was over, and the furnace could be shut down for the summer.*

I'll never forget my first encounter with the "dentist door," which is what we called the swinging door between the kitchen and the living room. When we kids had a loose "baby tooth," we would assist each other in the "extraction." First, you took some of Mom's thread and tied a knot around the loose tooth, and then tied the other end of the thread to the doorknob on the swinging door. Your brother or sister then played the part of the "dentist." Playing the dentist was the best part because you got to swing the door in the opposite direction to rip the tooth out. I hated it when you went through the pain and the thread broke, and then you had to start all over again. The second attempt was more difficult because now you were in even more pain and bleeding all over the floor.

We walked about ten blocks to school in each direction, and the school was always open—even if a foot or more of snow came down. The only time the school would close was when coal for the school furnace ran out because the famous union boss, John L. Lewis, called a coal miner's strike. I don't think that happened very much during the war though.

The adults had an expression or saying to cover just about everything: Be a good boy. You go straight to school. You come straight home from school. You're a day late and a dollar short. That's a lot a' malarkey. You'd shake the morals of a saint. Go on, ya say. Get out a' here. How ya doin? Pay attention to your teacher. Remember the fourth commandment. Count yer blessings. That just goes to show ya'. Now don't be a wise guy. There's no sense in cryin' over spilt milk. Don't cross your bridges before you get to them, etc.

A familiar expression heard so often on the radio was: "We interrupt this program to bring you a special bulletin." The interruption was usually for news about a big battle happening somewhere in Europe or the Pacific, but sometimes it was to report that someone famous had died. One time In nineteen forty-four the news bulletin was about the death of Glenn Miller, the famous bandleader. Glenn was really popular because he had written so many special wartime songs that had a personal meaning for so many people. For that reason, even though no one actually knew him, the news of his death saddened all of the people who loved his music. The sadness was as strong as it might have been for someone losing a family member. His music had touched so many people's emotions, and now like so many other young men, he was taken away from us by the war. Music was extremely important to everyone during the war, because the songs were usually about a loved one far away from home. The priorities were your family, your friends, your religion, and your music. In that order—nothing was more important.

Although the streetcar or bus cost only five cents for adults, most people walked to wherever they were going because a nickel was considered a lot of money and could be better spent on clothes or food. My uncle Jim and DJ's father, Kevin Corrigan, would both walk the five miles in each direction to their jobs, and then meet after work for the walk home. Uncle Jim worked as a control tower operator for the railroad, while Mister Corrigan worked at the grain mill. Both jobs were down near the Buffalo River in the old First Ward where almost every blue-collar worker was of Irish descent. Regardless of weather conditions, both men walked through rain, snowstorms and sunny days to get to work. They went to work even when they were sick, and as they themselves would say, "That ain't nothin', not when all those boys are being wounded and dyin' on the other side of the world for us. They're the ones makin' the real sacrifice, not us. Besides, it's darned good exercise, ya know!"

Most workingmen from our neighborhood shared that attitude, and they also walked to work everyday. None of them thought that they were making a sacrifice. Mister Corrigan walked with Uncle Jim day after day until the lung disease had drained so much of his health that he was no longer able to go to work. When that happened, we began to worry about Uncle Jim making that ten-mile round-trip each day by himself, but that's not what bothered him.

"Kevin and I walked to work together for almost twenty years, and in all that time there wasn't more than a handful of days when we didn't meet at the corner. I got to know him like my own brother, and now it seems so darn lonely during that walk. I'm sure gonna miss him—an awful lot."

There would be other times later on, but that was the first time I had ever seen tears come into Uncle Jim's eyes. The second time was when he read the eulogy for Scoop at Saint Bridget's Church just a few months later. I can still recall the parting words to his good friend:

" . . . He was a decent man, a hardworkin' man. So long Scoop, old friend. I'm sure gonna miss ya. I'll be seein' ya . . . And thanks for walkin' with me."

Uncle Jim continued to walk to work in all kinds of weather, all alone now, and I can still see him in his little black cord jacket and dark cap, lunch bucket tucked under his arm, leaning into the wind . . .

Fisty and I didn't know what to say to DJ because his father's death surprised us. We were always thinking the worst of possibilities about Joe, Phil, Tom, Jim, Gerry and my dad, so we just forgot that the civilians were also going to die. We didn't like talking about it around DJ because his voice would crack a little, and his eyes would fill up with tears. Besides, we didn't know what we could say that would be of any help.

"Jackie, what your uncle Jim said in church about my dad—that was really nice. I didn't know they were really close friends like that." DJ's voice cracked as he choked back a tear.

"Yeah, DJ, it was a nice talk, wasn't it?" The mood was awkward, and I was glad when DJ began talking about something more cheerful.

"Yer uncle Jim told me I could spend more time with you and him if I wanted to. He said he was already lookin' out for you because of yer dad being away in the war and everything. He says since you and me are good friends he figures it's a good idea. If that's okay with you?"

"It sure is, DJ. That's what friends are for, right! Besides, Uncle Jim's a good guy, ya' know. We can probably do some things together. And hey, you can come too, Fisty."

"Sure, that's okay with me you guys. I like Mister McDonald. He's kinda like my granddad who died couple a' years ago."

DJ started warming up to this new idea. "Hey, I got it, we can take him over to 'The Old Log' and he can go fishin' with us when Easter break starts. How 'bout that, huh?"

Fisty warmed to the idea, "Yeah, that's a good idea all right!"

DJ was an only child, probably because of the poor health of his dad, and now his mom was afraid of possibly losing their home. The mortgage payment was very difficult because she was employed as a "domestic," the term back then for a housekeeper. With the death of Mister Corrigan, life would be very tough for her and her nine-year-old son.

Having a job and owning a home were possibly the two most important goals in life. It was an almost sacred obligation to work to have a "home of your own." Owning a home, no matter how modest, had to do with your very identity as a person. In Ireland, so many people's homes and belongings were taken from them, and as a result of that bitter experience, they could never forget, even over generations, the bad memories of those times. Highest on the list of wrongs had been the confiscation of their small homes and farms by the British government during the days of "Penal Laws" and also following the uprising of seventeen ninety-eight. The psychological damage that had been done during those times went very deep into the grain, and would not be soon forgotten. They felt as though they had been stripped of their dignity. So to have had a small piece of property, and then to lose it would be like reliving the terrible memories of the past.

The neighbors on our street formed a committee to help Kitty Corrigan avoid the possible loss of her home. Uncle Jim, Father Johnny and Monsignor Foley were all involved right from the beginning with "The friends of Kitty," as the group became known. Donations came in right away to help her deal with the funeral expenses, and those donations came in the form of small amounts of change from hundreds of people all over the neighborhood. Then came the baked goods sales, newspaper drives, empty bottle collections for the penny deposit, and so many other activities that eventually there was enough money to pay the entire mortgage balance on the Corrigan home. It had only been about three months since the death of Scoop Corrigan when the house mortgage was paid in full. A small cake-and-coffee party was held at the church hall to mark the occasion. It was a very low-key affair involving just close friends and relatives. Respect for the family's pride was most important because people disliked the idea of having to accept charity—something looked upon as shameful. Of course, bragging about anything at all was absolutely despised. The identity of the hundreds, possibly thousands of donors was never divulged, nor was the amount of any individual donation ever revealed. The only certainty was that the donations were mostly from people of modest means themselves.

Uncle Joe gave Kitty a further boost when he told her, confidentially, that he had arranged for a job for her, and that it would pay more money to help with the maintenance expense of her home. The job was to be at his own place of employment at the big Curtis Airplane plant in Buffalo. At first she was concerned about having to travel so far to work on the streetcar. She had always worked at a doctor's home nearby, and that was just a short walk. Uncle Joe whispered something into her ear, and then swore her to secrecy about it. Whatever it was, she smiled as she looked over in the direction of our family.

-CHAPTER ELEVEN-

MOM BECOMES A "ROSIE"

"Guess what, kids? I've got a new job on the assembly line at the Curtis Airplane factory. I'll be working on fighter planes now, and making a bit more money ta boot!"

"Wow Mom, no kiddin'? You mean you're gonna be workin' on the famous P40? Wait till Dad hears about this, our mom helpin' to build the P40 fighter planes!"

"That's right, kids. Uncle Joe helped me get the job, and I'll be a trainee in his department. Not only that, but he was able to get a job for Kitty Corrigan too, and we'll be able to ride the bus together. I'm really excited about this 'cause maybe we can save a little more money towards buying this house someday so we won't have to rent anymore, or maybe get evicted and move away from our relatives. God, now wouldn't that be just wonderful." Mom's fondest dream for so many years was for us to have a "proper home of our own."

Mike said, "Well I'll be darned, our mom's gonna be a 'Rosie, the riveter!'"

"Rosie, the riveter" was the name used to describe the many thousands of women who went to work in the defense plants during the war. They were mostly housewives of all ages, some even grandmothers, who went to work in the factories to fill in for the shortage of men that came because of the war. These ladies, along with the men who were too old or not physically fit enough to be drafted, were not just filling the labor shortage gap. All of them "rose" to the occasion, working hard to make the necessary tools of war for our fighting men. They put in long hours doing work of the highest quality to make sure that our boys had the best equipment available. All around the country they helped to build airplanes, tanks, warships, cargo ships, jeeps, guns, ammunition and all of the hundreds of other goods necessary to fight such a big war. But the most important part of their work came from their attitude on the job. They were always aware of the need to do the very best job they were capable of doing, and that's something they didn't need to be told. Their job was a matter of deep, personal pride to them. They knew that their neighbor's sons, or possibly their own sons or husbands would be relying on the quality of each and every item they worked on. They had to be certain in their own mind that they had been meticulous and attentive to every detail in order to insure the highest degree of reliability possible. Their conscience would never allow otherwise. This was not just business, it was family, it was personal, and that's just the way it was.

"Okay now kids, Kitty and I will be workin' the afternoon shift, three to eleven, so I'll be dependin' on you, Margaret, to take care of supper for everyone. And I want everyone to help Margaret out with setting the table, washing dishes and anything else that needs to be done. I'll get the food ready before I leave for work, and that way it won't be such a burden if everyone cooperates. Okay? Anyone have any questions?"

"What about DJ, Mom; where will he eat if Mrs. Corrigan's at work?"

"Oh, yeah Jackie, I almost forgot; DJ will be coming over to our house to eat when Kitty's working."

"Hey Mom, that's great—all right!"

Margaret said, "Don't worry, you can depend on us, Mom. We'll be just fine."

"Sure, we'll all help out, Mom."

Mike said, "But Mom, what about when you and Mrs. Corrigan get off the bus so late at night? Should I come down to the corner and wait to walk you home?"

"Oh, Michael, I'm so glad you volunteered. That was what we were hoping, but we didn't want to interfere with your sleep."

"Well, I wouldn't be able to sleep anyway, not with worrying about you coming home so late, Mom."

"Okay then, I guess it's settled. Now is everyone sure this new job will be okay? If anyone's in disagreement then I won't do it."

"Au sure, Mom, we can do it!"

And that's why so much was accomplished—because of the teamwork and cooperation on the part of everyone in the families. Many of the mothers, including our own mother, even managed to find time for volunteer work in their free time. Mom, Aunt Mary, Margaret Mullaney and Kitty Corrigan volunteered their spare time to help out with Red Cross blood collections for the men in combat. They also baked cookies for packages and sent them to the men who didn't have someone to send them a package at Christmas time. They also wrote letters to those servicemen that didn't have anyone to write to them. It was a morale booster for those men, and because of it many long-term friendships were formed, which lasted long after the war was over. We received letters from former servicemen that came from all over the country after the end of the war, and one in particular I kept as a souvenir. It was the one letter that made all of us so proud of our mom.

Topeka, KANSAS
February 10, 1953

Dear Mrs. Rossiter,

I was just going through some mementos of my wartime experience, and I ran across your first letter from September 1944. As I re-read your letter I was still amazed at the insight and genuine concern that you had for me and my problems back then. There are some things that you can't say in life if you're not sincere. An impostor who fakes concern is always easy to spot. I just knew deep down in my heart and mind that you've never been into the business of being a phony person.

Your first letter arrived at a time when my outlook on life was very bleak, to say the least. I had been wounded on the first day of invasion at Normandy. I was with the army at a place called Omaha Beach where the scene was like one straight out of hell. As you know, I told you that my parents had died when I was very young, and I finished my early years in an orphanage so I didn't have any relatives to fall back on for moral support.

I've never told you this in my previous letters, but both of my legs had been shattered by a land mine, and they had to be amputated just above the knees. Because of the fierce gunfire coming from the German lines above us the medics couldn't get me off the beach for several hours. By then gangrene had set in, and afterwards onboard the hospital ship the doctors had to do several "resections" over the next couple of months. The doctors were finally able to control the infection, but when they tried to start my rehabilitation program I wasn't at all interested in artificial limbs. I was so far down into my own personal hell that I felt that I didn't have any reason to live, let alone walk again—but then your letters started coming.

Not only from what you said, but also the way you said it I could sense that you had possibly experienced a deep personal loss in the war. I had no way of knowing for certain; it was more of a feeling. I don't know why, but something between the lines of your words kept making me think, "This person seems to know about deep personal loss firsthand." If you decide that it's best not to tell me if my feelings were right, that's okay, I understand.

At any rate, your first letter began to lift my spirits. I found myself looking forward to your next letter, and I also began to think that maybe, just maybe I might be able to walk again someday.

Well, like they say, the rest is history now. Your letters of encouragement kept coming, and I eventually learned to walk on my artificial limbs. I went back to finish college, got my degree, then went on to medical school. I'm now a pediatrician with a practice here in Topeka. I love kids, and

now have three of my own. You know, I think about you
and your family almost everyday.

Thank God for all of the good people like yourself who
took the time to offer encouragement to us servicemen when
we so desperately needed it. Let's all hope and pray that our
own children never have to go through what we went
through. May God bless you and your family, Mrs. Rossiter.

Sincerely,

Doctor Sean McMahon

Yes, in just a few months' time something heartbreaking was
about to happen that would explain why our mom had been so
understanding to that wounded soldier in the late summer of
nineteen forty-four.

But in the meantime though, Mom and Mrs. Corrigan settled
into their new "Rosie" jobs while the war in the Pacific and Europe
dragged on through the start of a third year. There still wasn't any
word about Joe, so some of us were beginning to think the worst. Our
imaginations were beginning to get the best of us, but we could never
confirm our worst fears with words, so we kept our feelings to ourselves
and continued to pray for Joe and Dad, Jim, Phil, Tom, and Gerry
Mullaney—as well as all of the other servicemen.

My education about the war continued to grow with every
new place that I was hearing about. News of the battles came
about the Russians beginning to get the upper hand in their battles
against the Nazis, as well as the Nazi invasion of Hungary. In the
Pacific there was news of U.S. forces attacking Truk Island and
Kwajalein Atoll, and the Japanese crossing the border into India.
It was a very mixed picture so we couldn't see any advantage going
to either side. Everyone was becoming frustrated with the apparent
lack of progress in the war. We had no idea that something big was
about to happen very soon. The tone of the war would soon take a
dramatic turn. But for now it was the springtime, and all three of
us boys were looking forward to the Easter break from school.

At long last, a letter from Dad!

Dear Jackie,

I'm sorry it's been such a long time since my last letter. You see, I've been on all sorts of training missions, and I've also flown two real missions for the very first time.

Mom told me in her letters that your kidney treatment is coming along fine, and that it looks as if the doctors have it all under control because it was discovered so early. I can't begin to tell you how happy I was to hear that news. I just wish it were possible for me to be there to tell you that in person, Jackie. Now don't forget to take your medicine everyday, son.

From the sound of Mom's letters there's been all sorts of things happening at home. I felt bad about not being home for Johnny's ordination, but I did send him a note of congratulations. And it was really sad to hear about the death of Scoop Corrigan, our very good old friend. I tried for years to get him and Uncle Jim to ride to work on the bus, but they always wanted to walk. I can still recall one winter day when the snow was coming down and the wind was really blowing. The weather was just awful, but the both of them refused a ride. Couple a' real tough guys! I hope Uncle Jim doesn't keep walking by himself now that Scoop is gone.

I could hardly believe the news that Mom and Kitty Corrigan will be "Rosie, the riveters!" At first I was worried about her working so late, and in a factory so far away on the other side of town. But Mom told me about Mike waiting for them at the bus stop and how Uncle Joe will be watching out for them. Now I guess I'm not as worried as I was, but I told her to be real careful on the job because a factory can be a dangerous place to work if you don't always pay attention. Aw, I suppose she'll probably be okay. Buffalo is so far away, and I guess that's the real reason why I worry so much. I'm already looking forward to her next letter telling me about her new job, and I'm sure you kids are helping her out as much as you can.

Say, by the way, how's everything with that old furnace? Have you and Mike been able to take care of it without too much trouble? It's an old timer; so if you need any advice about anything just let me know, okay? And let me know if you need advice about anything else around the house. I know you both have a lot of responsibility now that I'm not home. I want you to know how much I appreciate everything you're doing to fill in for me, and how proud I am of the job that the both of you have been doing.

Jackie, as I told Mike in my letter to him, I'm going to tell you about some of my experiences over here now. Just like Mom was very honest with you so that your imagination wouldn't start painting exaggerated pictures, son, that's the way I want to be. Sometimes our imagination can make things seem worse than they really are.

First of all, the British people have been very friendly and they really appreciate our being here to help them win this war. I've made some friends from the Royal Air Force and I've found them to be pretty good guys. We trade stories about our families, so they know all about you, Mike and the girls. They talk with a funny accent, so I've had to get used to how they talk so I can understand them. They say they think that we're the ones with the funny accent. Almost all of the British people I've met have a relative or someone they know who's been injured or killed because of the war, so I guess we've been kind of fortunate. You know, whenever I see any young boys and girls over here I think of you boys and your sisters, and then I realize just how much I miss all of you.

My crew training was completed a few weeks ago and I've already been on two bombing missions. I can't tell you where those missions were located because of security reasons. I'm not going to tell you that the missions are easy because they aren't. The job is dangerous, and for that reason all the members of the crew are very close knit. We watch out for each other all the time. We've all realized (maybe for the first time in our lives) how important it is to pray to the Almighty, and I'm asking all of you kids to say a prayer for us everyday. This job over here is something I just felt that I had to do. I think a person needs to stand up for what you believe in. On the other hand, I hope the both of you boys never have to do anything like this.

I thought you might like to know the name that's on our plane. It's "Luck o' the Irish." Of course, it's painted in green and there's a big shamrock underneath. How 'bout that, huh! You see, the pilot and co-pilot are Irish, as well as the navigator and myself. The plane is brand-new and was brought over here just a few months ago. Captain Sullivan, the pilot, and Lieutenant Riley, the co-pilot, flew the plane over here from the States. Since they were the first to fly the plane they were given the right to name it. The name makes us Irish feel very proud. The rest of the crewmen are Italian, Polish, French and German decent. Yes, that's right, I did say German decent, but like the rest of us we're all Americans now. We all know how fortunate we are to be living in a free country. All of us are doing something very important together that we know is right. And besides, we all have to depend on each other if we're ever gonna get this war over with.

Well, I've gotta run now—lots of work to do on the plane because we all help with maintenance when we're not flying. Say a prayer for me, and I'll say one for you. Oh, and by the way, I wrote a letter to DJ about his dad and how I remembered Scoop. Tell DJ how glad I am that he's been coming over for dinner now, and how Mom says that she's also going to invite Mrs. Corrigan. They're both welcome in our home anytime. DJ should get the letter about the same time as you get this one. I hope it cheers him up a little. And by the way, that was a fine thing that everyone did for Mrs. Corrigan, paying off the funeral bills and the house mortgage like that. We know it can never replace Scoop, but it must have made her feel good to know how many people love her at a time like that. Boys, our family has been blessed by one

of the most important things in life—good friends. Always
remember that.

How's everything goin' with the baseball, Mike? Are
the scouts still comin' around to watch these days? You must
be ready for the new season by now, huh? Keep a sharp eye
out for the guy tryin' ta steal second! God bless you and
Jackie. Take good care of Mom and the girls for me. Don't
forget that you and Jackie are the men of the house now.

Love, Dad

P.S. Jackie, check with Uncle Jim. I think there's a special
surprise package there for you. And say a prayer everyday
for Jim, Joe, Phil, Tom and me. We all need your help.

"Wow Uncle Jim, it's the model airplane kit I was savin' up for,
the B-17 just like Dad flies in." I ran my fingers across the soft
Balsa wood that I'd be working with. "How did Dad find something
like this in England?"

"Well, he didn't, Jackie. He told me to check on the price, and
we bought it down at the hobby shop on Seneca Street. I hope ya
like it."

"Oh, I sure do Uncle Jim. I better write Dad a letter real soon
so I can tell him thanks."

"Now Jackie, if you need any help with puttin' the model
together I'll give ya a hand. I did a little model buildin' myself—
course it was many years ago.

"Oh, and by the way Jackie, how'd ya like to go to work with
me on the railroad while you're off from school during Easter break?
Your mom says it would be okay with her." I could hardly believe
what I was hearing.

"Go to work with you? On the railroad? For the whole eight hours?"

"That's right son, and you can bring a lunch just like I do. I'll
show ya what railroadin's all about. Now I'm back on the day shift,
seven to three since my friend Scoop passed away, so you'll have to get
up early. Okay?" My first trip to the railroad would prove to be the
beginning of a new and different world of adventure for me.

-CHAPTER TWELVE-

THE RAILROAD WORKERS

The first control tower that Uncle Jim took me to work at was a place called "River Bridge," where there were two primary responsibilities. The first job was to control the work engines coming in and out of the freight yard onto the main line tracks. The second job was operating the huge lift bridge over the river to let the big Great Lakes freighters travel up and down the river as they picked up and delivered goods to the many industries. Wow, what a perfect place of adventure for a nine-year-old boy!

As we walked to work that first day through the famous area known as "The Ward," Uncle Jim told me all about the history of that earliest part of our city. In the eighteen hundreds most of the blue-collar workers were Irish immigrants who had come to the U.S. because of the great famine in Ireland. These immigrants had limited skills and education, and so they provided most of the hard labor for the building of such big projects as the transcontinental railroads, the Tennessee Valley Power Project and digging The Erie Canal. The western end of the Erie Canal was of course, Buffalo, so it was the logical place where these former laborers would settle down and go to work at the various jobs created by the completion of the canal.

The city became a grain milling and storage hub, a railroad center and a port city. Then followed the many jobs involved in the grain business, the longshoremen and ships crews, and of course the thousands of railroad jobs. The news of work being available spread back to Ireland through the immigrants' letters, and this in turn brought even more Irish immigrants to the area. These people tended to settle close to the work places, and that's why there were so many homes scattered amongst the industrial buildings that followed. Later years brought more industry such as chemical, steel and auto plants. Then during the war, the aircraft and defense industry became a source of even more jobs. That's when the city became an industrial powerhouse.

The toughest part of The Ward was an area known as "The Valley," which we had to walk through to get to the railroad tower. I had heard and experienced enough to know that I was a little apprehensive about walking through that part of the city, but Uncle Jim put my mind at ease right away.

"Now Jackie, that's not a problem 'cause I'm real well known around here after all these years, you'll see. Besides, we're Irish too, ya' know!" Well, we must have had at least thirty friendly people speak to us along the way.

"Hey, Jimmy, how ya' doin'? Who's the new worker ya' got in tow?"

"He's a little young ta be railroadin', ain't he, Jimmy?"

"How ya doin', Jimmy? That yer grandson?"

"Gonna teach him the ropes, huh Jimmy!"

"Hi ya Jimmy. Sorry ta hear about Scoop Corrigan. Damn shame, that black lung thing."

"How ya doin', son? Now don't you go workin' in those grain mills, ya hear!"

As we walked along, I told him about the two bullies in Caz Park who were from "The Ward." He got quite a kick out of Fisty scaring them off.

"That's the only way ta do with their kind, don't let 'em get an inch or they're gonna want a mile. This neighborhood is known for bein' tough, but the real tough guys are the ones who get up and go to work everyday—even when they don't feel good. Gol darn it, they're the real tough people, Jackie, not those little punks. Most of the people in this neighborhood are good people who've had a tough life, that's all." I began to feel very safe just being around this wise man, and by the time we were just a few minutes from the control tower, I had forgotten all about Peewee Hayes and Butch Ryan.

The control tower was a tall, red-brick building overlooking the nearby Buffalo River. There were two sets of main-line railroad tracks in front of the building. Uncle Jim explained that one track was for eastbound trains, the other for westbound. The tower appeared larger still because the tracks were up at the top of a hill about twenty feet above the parking area that we walked through on the way. About eighty feet to the left of the tower stood a monstrous, counterweight bridge. As we walked up the incline and came closer to the bridge it seemed even bigger to me. I was in awe of such a large mass of concrete and steel, and I was intimidated by the immensity. The bridge, the railroad tracks, the wide river and the very high control tower were all very exciting to me. I could feel my heart beating faster, so I stayed as close as I could to Uncle Jim.

We crossed the two sets of tracks and walked up a double flight of stairs on the outside of the building to get to the entrance door. Before crossing the tracks, I was given my first lesson in safety. "Stop, look both ways and listen before ya cross over railroad tracks, Jackie. If you tangle with one of these machines you'll be killed for sure. No second chances here, ya know."

The inside of the tower had large windows so that you had a good view in every direction from this perch about twenty-five feet above the tracks. Uncle Jim was "relieving" the night shift worker, an elderly man with gray hair and thick glasses.

"Who's this with ya, Jimmy? A new trainee?" He flashed a smile as he said that.

"Tommy, this is my nephew, Jackie Rossiter, I been tellin' ya all about. He's gonna be postin' the job, so you'd best look out for the new job competition." The both of them were grinning to each other. I later learned that "posting" was a term for a new employee in training.

"Jackie, say hello to Mister Milligan."

"Hello, Mister Milligan, sir."

The gray-haired man put his hand into mine and said, "Hello, Jackie. Welcome to the River Bridge Control Tower. I'll bet you're gonna like this place—I just know you will."

Both men went to the desk in the middle of the tower and began to discuss the changing of the shift responsibility over to Uncle Jim. "Now Jim, the *Cornelius Boland* went upriver to The Socony Refinery about three hours ago, so she'll probably be comin' back down soon. Then there's the Ashtabula coal train. It was announced in by Erie dispatch just a few minutes ago, so he'll need the signal soon. And, oh yeah, job ten, Buffalo Yard wants to come out for the Concrete Elevators at about eight o'clock, but Jack O'Shea said he'll call when he's ready. I haven't heard number fifty-one announced out of the terminal yet."

As the two men talked, I glanced around at the overhead electronic control panel that looked like a big relief map with red and green lights blinking. It had a black background with two sets of white tracks running from end to end across it. Underneath the control panel was a large bank of red, pistol-grip style handles on a big console that electronically controlled all of the switches and signals. At the end of the tower towards the river was a different-looking control panel with all sorts of gauges and instruments. It was in front of a large window that looked out on that huge bridge and the river. I figured that must be the bridge-opening controls. Wow! What a complicated-looking thing, I thought. My mind was overwhelmed with all of these strange-looking machines.

"Tommy, did you say Jack O'Shea's on job ten today?"

"He sure is, and just as funny as ever, Jimmy."

My uncle turned to me and said, "Jackie, wait till ya hear Jack O'Shea—He's one in a million all right!"

Pretty soon Mister Milligan was leaving, and then Uncle Jim sat down at the big desk overlooking the front of the tower. He pushed down on a foot pedal under the desk and said into a big speaker, "Hello, Buffalo Dispatch, River Bridge checking in, start of shift." The dispatcher's reply could be heard over the speaker loud and clear in the entire tower. In fact, all conversation from each and every tower, as well as conversation from the terminal dispatcher could be heard in all of the control towers. Because it was an intercom set up, all news was heard simultaneously by all of the control tower operators. That system meant that everyone concerned was up to date on all train movements on the entire Buffalo Division. The Chief dispatcher at the terminal had overall authority. In Uncle Jim's words, "He's the 'honcho.'"

"Hello, River Bridge. Buffalo Dispatch acknowledges. Good mornin' Jimmy. How ya' doin'?"

"Okay, Pat. Say, how's number fifty-one doin'? Little late today, huh?"

"He's on his air right now, Jimmy. I should be announcin' him out any minute now. Let's see here, yeah, he's runnin' about four minutes late, so give him the highball and let him go. He can make up that time easy between here and Cleveland."

"On his air" meant that the engineer was pumping up the air through the hose connections on the entire train in order to release the brakes on all of the cars. Being "announced out" meant that the dispatcher at the terminal was giving permission for the train to depart through the use of remote electronic signals alongside the tracks. When that occurred he was passing responsibility for the train to all of the control towers along the way. The first tower to take responsibility gave the green signal to the approaching train by also using remote electronic signals from that tower.

"Highball" was a term used in giving the highest priority green signal to increase speed rapidly. Each subsequent control tower would "announce" the train into the next control tower down the line, and so on. When the train would enter what was called your "block" of responsibility, you were then required to watch the passing train for any mechanical problems. Some possible problems might include the brake rigging coming loose on an individual car, or a "hot journal." A hot journal was when a wheel bearing overheated and started smoking due to a lack of lubrication on the bearings.

These were really dangerous defects because a derailment could occur—something so serious that no one ever wanted to be responsible for that happening. If a derailment occurred, even at low speed, loss of life and heavy property damage could be the result. At high speed, the result could resemble a war-zone explosion. When a serious mechanical defect was spotted, the next tower operator along the line would be alerted through the intercom phone so that they could "swing him up." That was the term used to stop the train immediately, either through the electronic signals or through manual hand signals. Of course it took me a long time to understand all of that exciting talk. I learned right away that I was going to be known to everyone as "Kid." That name was used just a few minutes later when the famous conductor of job ten, Jack O'Shea called in on a separate intercom,

"Hey Jimmy, is that you? You old Mick, I hear tell if ya shake yer family tree some Polish and "Eye-talian" ancestors just might fall out on the ground. Would that be true now?"

"Jack, who you kiddin'? I hear yer family dropped the "ski" when they got off the boat!"

"Au, Jimmy, I'm only joshin' ya. But accordin' ta very reliable sources yer own mother said the map of Ireland was written all over that puss a' yer's. 'Course, maybe the map was showin' all those Irish peat bogs, huh?"

"Now Jack, best be warned you'll have to watch the language today, 'cause my young nephew is postin' the job here."

"Is that right? Say kid, how ya doin'? Yer uncle's been braggin' about ya comin' ta work fer weeks now. Now see here Kid, don't ever be a tower-operator like Jimmy. Get yerself a real job: Be a conductor like me, kid!"

"Hello, Mister O'Shea, sir."

"Oh, good Lord, whady'a know, a polite kid. Are ya sure he's yer kin, Jimmy? Say Kid, Jimmy tells me yer dad's a crewmember on a bomber in England. How's he doin? Do ya write to him now and then?"

"Yeah, I write to him every week, Mister O'Shea. And he writes back to me a lot, too."

"Well, the next time you write to him I want ya to tell him Jack O'Shea says hello and God bless. Ya see I met yer dad many years ago when he first came ta this country. You can be real proud of him, Jackie. You know that now, don't ya?"

"Yes sir, I sure do."

"All right, enough a' this socializin', we gotta get some work done, Kid. Okay now, Jimmy, gimme the green into the "Concrete." (The Concrete Grain Elevator Company.) We gotta make up an out bound fer Chicago."

"Are you still playin' that old sandbag game of yours, Jack? You know darn well I can't give ya the green while the 'fleet's' runnin'." The "fleet" was the name for the sleek passenger trains going west to Chicago and east to Buffalo at that time of day. O'Shea would always wait until the main line traffic became the busiest before calling in for clearance—knowing in advance that he couldn't get that clearance. Of course, that meant an hour's wait—which was an opportunity for the entire crew to take a nap. Uncle Jim had no choice but to go along with the charade.

"Look Jack, why not take a break and I'll ring ya up when the main line quiets down—just like we always do, right?"

"Well now, if you insist Jimmy. You're the boss man. And say, if that 'Eye-talian' yardmaster calls and inquires about us, you give him plenty a' malarkey now. Drive him good and nuts, okay? Oh, and by the way, all the 'Sons a' Erin' here on the crew said ta say hello. You keep the faith now, ya hear?"

"Pleasant dreams, Jack."

"Now watch over there, Jackie, you'll be seein' a salute any minute now." Sure enough, the window on the caboose opened and an arm came out with a "thumbs-up" signal, and then the arm was retracted back into the caboose and the window closed again. I never did get to meet Jack O'Shea, or see his face, just his arm and thumb signal, but I was going to hear plenty of his jokes over the intercom. I guess the mystery of wondering what he might look like stirred my curiosity about the man. About that time the loud speaker began to come alive with news of main-line trains approaching.

"Hello, River Bridge, this is Exchange Street. Number fifty-one comin' out of the terminal on track one. Open up the gates and let 'em highball."

"River Bridge, got it, 'EX'. Comin' at ya Bufflo Creek."

"Buff'lo Creek here—got it, Jimmy. Very often people would drop the "a" sound in the word Buffalo. In fact, many Buffalonians still have that habit to this day.

Uncle Jim showed me how he was giving the green signal to the westbound passenger train by pulling out one of the pistol grip devices. After he pulled the handle out a green light came on at the far-left end of the relief map up above. After a couple of minutes there was a short bell sound, and a white light came on at the far left side of the map. He explained that this indicated the location of number fifty-one entering his block, and we had to get ready to inspect the train as it went past the tower. Before fifty-one was in sight though, the tower to the west announced, "Hello, River Bridge, this is Buffalo Creek Tower. Ashtabula coal train comin' at ya on track two—open the gates, Jimmy!"

"Okay, Buffalo Creek. Got it, Paddy. Exchange Street, did ya hear that? Ashtabula coal train on the way, track two."

"Ex. Got it, Jimmy."

Then he pulled out the red-handled control to give the green indication to the eastbound freight train. Suddenly there was a lot of activity after having been real quiet. Then Uncle Jim said, "Okay Jackie, here we go, there's fifty-one roundin' the bend at Buff'lo Yard."

The excitement was building up inside me as the passenger train, being pulled by new diesel locomotives, rounded the bend towards the tower. Then in a flash the train was heading past the tower, accelerating rapidly. The noise was deafening. The building shook as that huge machine came so close, and then the loud sound of the "clickety—clack" of the wheels on the track made it seem like the train was actually inside the tower. I watched as it passed by with a blur, and I caught just a glimpse of people having breakfast in a dining car. In only an instant it had come and then just as quickly it was gone. I stood there motionless with my mind in a blank as I watched the rear of the last car disappear across the bridge to our right. My face was still warm with all this excitement and fear as I watched my uncle write the time data into a big ledger book. Then he went to the control panel and returned the westbound green signal indication to the red position, which put the red signal back on the block.

"Well Jackie, whaddya think?"

All that I could say was, "Wow!"

"Kinda figured you'd say that the first time. Were ya scared?"

"A little. No, a lot, I guess."

"You gonna be all right, son? Ya look a little pale." I nodded yes.

"Well, not much time to think about it, 'cause here comes the Ashtabula coal train on track two now."

This was a very long freight train of about one hundred and twenty cars of heavy coal, and it was being pulled by a giant steam engine. There was the unmistakable "ch-ch-ch" sound coming from the steam-driven cylinders, and a plume of dark gray smoke was spewing from the funnel on top of the engine. This was the engine right out of the western movies. This was the engine that little boys and grown-up men saw in their imagination whenever the word "railroad" was mentioned. This was the locomotive associated with thoughts of the eighteen hundreds. The coal train was beginning to slow down on the way into the steel plants in Buffalo, so the sound was different from the accelerating passenger train. This train was really heavy, about ten thousand tons, causing the ground to rumble, and the tower began to shake as it chugged across the bridge. When it was in front of the tower, the engineer waved to us, and for the first time I felt a close connection with the people actually operating the trains. Being connected with the people they called the "operating" crew made me feel real important. The ground and the tower began shaking as if there was an earthquake until the train was well past the tower. The noise was deafening as it rumbled past us. From the caboose window at the rear, the conductor gave us a thumbs-up signal, and we both waved back to him. I continued to watch in fascination as the caboose disappeared around the bend near the Buffalo Yard. That was my first railroading experience, and it was intoxicating stuff for a young boy.

Uncle Jim returned the signal to the red position, and then gave me some more lessons about railroading as a steady stream of other trains went speeding past the tower. Finally, after the main-line traffic had quieted down, he rang the yard phone near job ten. After several rings, we could hear the groggy sound of Jack O'Shea's voice.

"Jeez, Jimmy, you got no heart wakin' up a bunch a' honest-workin' men like that."

"Rise and shine, sweetheart. Time to get some work done."

"Okay, okay, Jimmy. Give us the green so's we can get into the Concrete Grain Elevators and take our break now!"

"Jack, yer a real beaut!"

"Hey, now wait a darned minute here. First ya call me sweetheart, and then ya say I'm beautiful. Yer not one of those funny guys, are ya? Wait till I tell all the guys about this now!"

"There's the green, Jack. You guys had better be gettin' some work done or we'll all be in the hot water."

"Yeah, yer right Jimmy, but say, before I forget, has there been any news about young Joe Rossiter? Me and the crew are always thinkin' about him, ya know."

"No, still no news, Jack. We all wish there was, but thanks fer askin'."

"Well, we'll all be sayin' one for him to come home safe, Jimmy. Oh, and we'll also be sayin' one fer young Jimmy. Tell me, is he okay, and where in the world is he servin' these days?"

"He's fightin' the Germans in northern Italy, along with Phil and Tommy Rossiter, Joe's brothers. The three boys are okay, thank God. Thanks fer askin', and God bless you and the boys, Jack."

"Oh, all of us guys on the crew just wish this damn war was over, and the boys could all come back home, Jimmy. It just seems ta drag on forever. Well, we gotta run. Be seein' ya, Jimmy. See ya, Kid. Now don't be forgettin', say hello to yer dad for me, ya hear? And we'll be sayin' one fer him, too, Jackie!"

As the yard engine and caboose rolled west past the tower, there was a blast of the air horn and Jack O'Shea's thumbs-up signal came out the window again—but still no sight of that comical character. Then my thoughts about the mysterious comedian came to a sudden halt as I was scared stiff by an *extremely* loud blast of the air horns on the six hundred-foot ship called *The Cornelius Boland*. It was on its way downriver, and they were signaling for the bridge to be opened up.

"Hello, Buffalo Dispatch, this is River Bridge requesting permission to open the bridge."

"How long ya need, Jimmy?"

"Oh, about ten minutes, Pat."

"All right then, go ahead Jimmy. You got it."

The first thing that Uncle Jim did was to press a large button that started loud bells and sirens warning anyone who might be walking across the bridge. As he went through the procedures at the large console he explained each step along the way.

"First we retract the bridge locks, then we slowly apply electrical current to start the bridge goin' up. Ya have to be careful not to apply too much power 'cause that could be dangerous. There's plenty extra power in case it's needed for high wind or somethin'. Now we watch the degree of open gauge—that big round one in the center of the console." He pointed in that direction. "Then we have to make sure that the bridge is fully open, not just by lookin' at the degree reading, but by actually watchin' the bridge open up. If the bridge starts goin' too fast there's two sets a' brakes that we use, but that's mostly used when you're takin' the bridge back down."

I was thinking how businesslike and serious Uncle Jim was while explaining the bridge operation procedure, but I was also keeping an eye on the rotating bridge. It seemed impossible for something so big to be going up so easily. The huge concrete counterweight came down in an arcing motion, almost touching the rails as the steel bridge deck, train rails and all, went straight up about a hundred feet in the air. Then we heard two blasts from the giant freighter's air horns as the bow of the ship slowly appeared in front of our window. Crewmembers on deck were waving to us, and as we waved back, Uncle Jim wondered, as though to himself, where they were bound for. His voice sounded wistful, and I suspected that he wanted to be on that big ship himself.

"You know about how yer dad sailed the Great Lakes when he first came to the U.S. from Canada, don't ya Jackie? Yer dad knows a lot about ships and sailin'."

"Yeah, he told me that once, Uncle Jim. Did you ever sail on a ship?"

"No, never did, but I often wondered how it'd be. Must be somethin' out of our Irish past, the love of the sea I mean. I guess so many Irish were involved with the sea, maybe 'cause most of them lived near the coast back in the old country. Some things in life are in the blood, I guess; that's somethin' that doesn't go away easy ya' know."

He closed the big bridge after the *Boland* had cleared, then continued standing in front of the window, staring out across the river at the tall cylinders of the Concrete Grain Elevators. He was very quiet for a long moment, and then began to talk about his old friend while still staring at the grain elevators. "That's where DJ's dad worked for so many years, Jackie. He used to walk across this bridge after I came up to the tower, and then at quit time I'd wait for him to come back across the bridge for our walk home. Sometimes I can still see him walkin' this way down the tracks after work, all the while wavin' ta me."

He kept staring through the window, and seemed lost in his thoughts until the voice from the speaker said: "Hello, River Bridge, Buff'lo Dispatch here. Jimmy, how's that big boat comin' along? Is he clear yet Jimmy? 'Cause we got a high-priority freight train comin' through from the east."

"Yeah, Pat, he's all clear and the bridge is down and locked. What's this high-priority stuff all about?"

"It's a special load of important military equipment headed for the West Coast. I guess it's for the war in the Pacific, Jimmy. Anyway, this guy's got the highest priority over all other trains— all the way ta' San Francisco. They call it train number 'W-E-1.' They tell me the W-E stands for War Effort."

"Sounds like he's in a big hurry, huh Pat?"

"Yeah Jimmy, so 'Katy bar the door' on everything else, no matter what. Give this guy the green right away and let him highball!"

"Gotcha Pat, will do!"

We could hear Pat the dispatcher giving the same orders to all of the other control towers all the way to the end of the Buffalo Division at Bay View Tower. The Bay View Tower would then announce that same information to the Erie, Pennsylvania dispatcher, and so on down the line. That's the way the operation worked: The various divisions on the main-line tracks would control all trains, and pass them through to the next division until that train eventually reached its final destination. That's when the train would be switched into a freight yard for final delivery to wherever the freight was being shipped to.

We watched in silence as the special freight train passed by on the way to San Francisco, a city that I had only seen on a map. There were mostly boxcars, but there were also a number of flatbed cars loaded with new tanks, armored cars and big artillery guns covered with canvas. These weapons were being sent to the Pacific to be used where my cousin Joe, and DJ's brother Gerry were. I couldn't help but think of our friends and relatives in the military as I watched the last car disappear across the bridge. Uncle Jim must have had those same thoughts.

"Let's hope that equipment helps the boys end that war over there, so they can all come back home, Jackie." Reminders of the war were everywhere.

By quitting time when we were relieved for shift change, I had learned more in those eight hours than I could have ever imagined. My mind was crammed full of what I had seen and heard as I tried to fall asleep that night. I've always remembered my first day's experience with life on the railroad, and although I didn't realize it then, that day would prove to be the first day of a life-long fascination and fondness for the people and the machinery of that unique profession.

> *Dear Dad,*
>
> Wow, thanks a lot! Uncle Jim gave me the model airplane kit that you and him got for me. He helped me put the bomber together. It was fun doing it, and now I know a lot

about the B-17 that you fly in. I just wish you could be here
to help me put it together. Well, you know. I hope you're real
safe and okay when you get this letter, Dad! Everybody here
is okay, and all us kids help out at home now that Mom is
working such a hard job. Margaret looks out for us, especially
Mary and me. Sometimes she tries to lie to us about the time
on the clock after supper when it's time to come home to go
to bed. She can't do that anymore though 'cause I learned
how to tell the time myself now. But she's okay for a girl, I
guess.

I bet you probably heard from Mom how Uncle Jim
has been taking me to work on the railroad. Boy, it sure is
fun over there. I talked to a Mister Jack O'Shea, and he says
to say hello to you and how ya doin'. He said he knew you
when you first came to America. He hopes you're okay. He
says that you're a good man, but we already knew that, Dad.
There's this really neat place called River Bridge where Uncle
Jim showed me how to lift the big bridge over the river. I
saw a six hundred-foot boat go by, and Uncle Jim says you
really know a lot about big ships and sailing. When you
come home I want you to tell me all about that stuff, okay?

Uncle Jim showed me the place where DJ's father used
to work. It's just across the river from the tower, and Uncle
Jim feels really bad every time he looks over that way. He
stares over there for a long time, and doesn't say anything at
all. I can tell he misses Mister Corrigan a lot. When we walk
to work everybody says hello and how ya doin to Uncle Jim.
He sure knows lots of nice people.

Thanks for tellin' me all about your job in the bomber,
and all about the English people, Dad. It must be exciting
what you do, but I really worry a lot about if you're okay and
everything, you know. Aunt Mary showed me where
Alconbury is on the big map. It sure is a long ways away. I
wish I could see what it looks like over there.

Don't worry, the furnace is workin' okay. Mike and me
take turns shovelin' the coal and everything. I get kinda

scared when I go down in the cellar at night. The coal bin is spooky, but Mike laughs and says it's only my imagination. Hey, guess what. Uncle Jim is gonna come fishin' at "The Old Log" with Fisty, DJ and me. How 'bout that, huh? He says he used to go fishin' when he was young like us, and now he misses it a lot. I'm really glad Uncle Jim is here with me since you're so far away. He's a neat guy. Even Fisty and DJ said so. DJ got your letter about his dad. He didn't tell us what you said, and he cries a lot when he talks about it so we don't say too much anymore because we don't want to make him feel bad. DJ said to tell you thanks a lot.

I only have to go to the hospital once a month now and I still see Doc Carden once a month too. He says to tell you to keep your head down and he'll say a prayer for you. Lots of people in the neighborhood ask me how ya doin'. They said they'd say a prayer for you, too. We all miss you a lot, Dad. By the way, did you hear the good news about Father Johnny? He's gonna stay at Saint Bridget's for good now 'cause the other assistant priest went into the army. Everybody is really happy about that. We all say prayers at church for you and Joe, Jimmy, Phil and Tom. Be real careful, Dad. See ya!

Love, Jackie

-CHAPTER THIRTEEN-

FLY RODS AND STEAM ENGINES

When the day came to go fishing with Uncle Jim, all three of us boys were so excited that we weren't able to sleep, so we were waiting on his front porch before the sun came up. We were really anxious to show him our secret spot at "The Old Log." He came out on the porch with a big smile, and I think he was just as excited as we were.

"Mornin' men. Who's gonna catch the big one today?"

Fisty said, "What the heck's that kind a' fishin' pole, Mister McDonald? I never saw one like that before." Uncle Jim had a pole in his hand that must have been ten feet long.

"Fisty, this is called a fly rod; it's normally used ta catch trout in small streams, but you can use it fer Black Bass in creeks too. It's made out a' bamboo."

As we walked along Seneca Street I was still curious about that pole. "Uncle Jim, how come it's so long?"

"That's 'cause ya' don't cast by usin' the reel, Jackie. You work the line out a little at a time in your hand, then ya' use the long pole to kinda whip the line out where you want it to go. You need to keep workin' the line in the direction of the spot ya' want. It'll be easier to show ya' what I mean when we get there."

"Say, I'll bet you boys haven't had any breakfast. How 'bout if we stop for some hot cross buns and chocolate milk at Miller's Bakery? Whaddya say?"

"Yeah, that sounds good, Uncle Jim!" We gobbled down the food as we walked through the park towards our "secret" spot at "The Old Log." It was a cool spring morning, the sun was beginning to warm us, and I felt really excited at the thought of the day ahead. I only wished that Dad, and Joe, and Jim, and Gerry, and Phil and Tom could be suddenly and magically with us. I wished that the stupid war would just stop and go away.

Uncle Jim worked himself down the incline of the creek bank, about sixty feet upstream from where we had dropped our lines into the water. We were about to tell him that the fishing was best where we were, as we were sure that we knew every little spot where the fish congregated around that Old Log. But, just watching the almost magical way that he worked that line back and forth through the early morning sunlight had us spellbound.

He had refused the juicy red worms that we'd found the night before—said he preferred something called a "Royal Coachman." We found it hard to believe that any fish was gonna go for somethin' that wasn't alive, but we remained quiet, and we watched with fascination as he began working the line towards an eddy just below a rock outcropping. His arm brought the line slowly backwards in a slow whip-type motion, and just before the artificial lure would reach its limits behind him, he would bring his arm forward toward the spot where he wanted the lure to go. The line was wet from hitting the water causing it to glisten in the morning sunlight as he worked it back and forth. It was almost magical to watch, as though he was pointing at the exact spot that he wanted just before the lure landed in the far end of the eddy. The current brought the artificial bug slowly across the still, deep water, and then suddenly the biggest Black Bass we had ever seen jumped clear out of the water. The green-colored giant came down headfirst on the "Royal Coachman," the water erupted, and the battle was on. That long pole bent so much that we thought the shaft was gonna break. Then suddenly there was a spectacular sight as the big fish came straight up out of the water, twisting and flinging itself high into the air, and then causing the water to erupt again as it came back down hard on the surface.

He kept adjusting the line in his fingers to keep it taut so that the fish would have no slack to maneuver its way off the hook. He had a real determined look on his face, and I could tell that he wasn't thinking about anything else but that big fish. He had to yell out at us to get the net ready because we had become so hypnotized by watching the entire spectacle. The battle probably took about three or four minutes, but it seemed more like twenty. As he held the line tightly he gave me instructions on how to properly use the net to land that huge fish. The netting of the fish was really difficult for me because I was actually afraid of that fish—something that I never dreamed could happen. I had fished for a few years already, but I had never been that close to such a large full-of-fight fish as that one.

"Holy smokes, Uncle Jim, that fish must be about eighteen inches and weighs maybe seven or eight pounds!"

"I'd say that's a fairly good guess, Jackie. It's a nice way ta start the day, especially since I been away from fishin' for several years now. What do you boys think of a fly rod now, huh?"

"Wow! That was the best fishin' I ever seen, Mister McDonald. Would you show us how to use that pole?"

"Sure would, DJ, but first let's put this fish back in the water."

"What! You mean you're gonna let that fish go?"

"Now don't get upset, Fisty. There's more where he came from. Besides, that fish is probably old like me so I want him to enjoy his time remainin' too. Ya gotta admit that he sure has a lot a' fight left in him, right?"

He spent the rest of the day showing us how to work the line on the fly rod, and explaining how the bait had to be "presented" on the water in just the right way. "You'll never fool trout or Black Bass unless ya learn ta first 'read' the water. Those fish are very shrewd, and can spot a phony real fast. They know if a bug on the surface of the water is doin' somethin' that's not right. Kinda like some people I've known over the years. Before you can catch 'em ya gotta know how they think 'cause they're not stupid. Now boys, take a lesson from that Big Bass: Even though he was old he didn't wanna quit, he kept fighting me all the way into the net—and he still fought me after he was in the net. He just refused ta give up, now didn't he?"

For the three of us boys, that was the beginning of a love affair with the fly rod. We promised ourselves that we'd start saving up right away so we could someday have one of our own. Fishing that way was so much more fun than simply hauling them in on a heavy line, a method that didn't require very much skill. On that day, in time, we all realized that he had not only taught us so much about a fascinating method of fishing; Uncle Jim had taught us so many principles about life itself. On that memorable day we all knew that something very special had taken place: Jim McDonald had become our mentor, friend and guardian.

But, just before we left "The Old Log," wouldn't you know it, "Vroom, vroom!" Pencil Dillon still lurks in the park! "Were you little punks swimmin' in the creek again? I figured I had all a' ya taken care of the last time."

"Well, waddya know, its Mickey Dillon himself! How ya been, kiddo?" Dillon hadn't seen Uncle Jim because he was folding up his gear about twenty feet away.

"Jimmy, old boy, what the heck are ya doin over here? I ain't seen ya around this place since I was a kid and you use to teach us how ta fish with a fly rod!"

The three of us boys looked at each other with shock and amazement. How was it possible that the guy we thought to be a non-member of the human race used to go fishing—and right here in *our* secret spot! We were stunned and just couldn't believe it.

"Well, Mickey, this here's my nephew, Jackie Rossiter, and the other two boys, DJ Corrigan and Fisty Mullaney are his friends. They come fishin' here sometimes, and they asked me if I'd come along with them, so here we are."

"Well now Jimmy, you know I had a few run-ins with these boys, and I gotta say, their manners were not the best I'm sorry ta say!"

"Yes, Tommy, I did hear about it, and I want you ta know that their fathers took the matter into their own hands—if you get my meanin'. And by the way, I think this is just the right time and place for these boys to be apologizin' to you directly fer not showin' the proper respect for your authority. Isn't that right now, boys?"

There we were offering apologies, not because we wanted to because of Dillon, but because of our respect for Uncle Jim. Our shock and surprise really sharpened when Dillon said:

"Say Jackie how's yer dad doin over there in England, flyin' in those bombers?"

I stammered, "Uh, he's doin' okay, sir." Now how the heck did he know about my dad being over there?

"DJ, I was real sorry ta hear about yer dad, Scoop. He was a good man, a hard-workin' man." DJ mumbled something, then put his head down.

"Fisty, how's young Gerry doin' in the Marine Corps? I hear he volunteered for the duty."

"Real good, officer Dillon. Thanks fer askin'."

As we stood there sneaking glances of surprise at each other, Dillon and Uncle Jim began talking to each other again. "Is there any word on young Joe these days, Jimmy? It seems like a long time since that news came around. And how's young Jimmy doin' in the army?"

"No, sorry ta say nothin' new on Joe, Mickey. And Jimmy's okay—so far, anyway. He's in the infantry, fightin' in Italy now. Say, how's young Pat doin' in the navy these days? I hear he's been servin' on a destroyer in the Pacific. Is that right?"

"Yeah, that's true, Jimmy. He's in charge of an anti-aircraft gun, and he's a fair mechanic so he fills in with the engine room crew too. Katherine and I are always worried about him 'cause he's so young to be over there, just eighteen ya' know."

"Yer only boy, right?"

"That's right, Jimmy, he is."

"We'll say one for him, Mickey."

We couldn't believe what we were hearing because we had always looked upon Dillon as our enemy. He seemed to be always showing up to spoil our fun just as we were starting to have a good time swimming in the creek. That last comment from Uncle Jim about a prayer caused Dillon's voice to break a little. I thought he became a little embarrassed.

"Jimmy, it's been a real pleasure seein' ya again. Say hello ta all the folks for me, will ya now. And you boys now don't be swimmin' in that creek anymore. It's real dangerous—I know! See ya men!" Vroom, vroom!

Fisty said, "Wow, did you hear that? Holy smokes, he called us '*men*'!"

Uncle Jim picked up his gear, and then said, "Come on guys, I've got some things ta tell ya on the way home."

As we made our way out of the park and down Seneca Street, Uncle Jim told us a fascinating story about Dillon that gave us feelings of guilt and surprise. "Boys, round about the time I was oh, about twenty-seven, back in nineteen twenty was the first time I ever met Mickey. Margaret and I use ta come ta 'Bufflo' for a visit with my Sister Mary's family. Back then they lived on Good Avenue, right near Caz Creek. Now my dad had taught me how ta fish with a fly rod when I was a boy, so I always brought my pole along ta fish in Caz for a while. Well, one day while I'm fishin', this fifteen-year-old boy comes up and starts askin' questions about my fly rod, and how he'd never seen anyone use that kinda pole before." Uncle Jim looked me straight in the eye as he said, "'Bout the same kind a' questions that you were askin' me this mornin', Jackie." I suspected what might be coming next, so I looked down towards the ground.

"Well, I learned that this young boy's name was Mickey Dillon, and him and I became good friends 'cause of our love for fishin'. Every time I'd come ta Buffalo we'd meet right down there near that Old Log where we spent many hours together, just talkin' about life and fishin'." All that I could think was: At *our* Old Log! The three of us boys were stealing glances at each other. The feeling of surprise and guilt was growing stronger for all of us.

"Well, then one day Mickey brings his nine-year-old brother along. Says would I mind if Kevin learned how ta fish with a flyrod? No problem, I said. Kevin was a pretty fast learner, and I think he had a bit of natural ability. We fished fer several hours that day, and then I had ta go back ta Binghamton the next mornin'. I gave them both one a' my hand-tied flies, then said 'so long 'till next time'. At this point he paused for a few minutes, and just stared straight ahead while we continued walking in silence towards home. After a few minutes he took a deep breath, and then exhaled. He had a pained look on his face now.

"Well, I didn't come back for a visit till that September, and when I went down ta go fishin' again, Mickey and Kevin weren't there. I learned from some guys fishin' nearby that young Kevin had drowned while swimmin' near that Ol' Log only two days before. I went right over ta Loomis funeral home that afternoon, and by God I wanna tell ya that was one of the hardest things I ever had to do in my life, boys." He again paused in silence as we continued walking towards home. He had a look of pain on his face, and I began to have feelings of guilt because of how we had treated Dillon. I was slowly beginning to understand why he had been so intense about keeping us from swimming in that creek.

"So ya see boys, every time he sees you boys swimmin' in that creek, he's really seein' Kevin all over again. He just can't help it, he's convinced that someone else who's about nine years old or so is gonna drown down there again. He still blames himself for his brother's death, ya see."

I said quietly, "We didn't know about that, Uncle Jim."

"I know ya didn't boys. It's a long time ago, and no one wants ta talk about it anymore 'cause it's a bad memory. Now, what I'd like you boys ta do is say a prayer once in a while for both Kevin, and Mickey's son, Patrick . . . Okay, guys?"

By this time we had become quiet and thoughtful. None of us wanted to say anything, so we just nodded to Uncle Jim. In the days that followed we often talked with each other about what we had learned that day, but as time went by we stopped talking about it. We learned that sometimes people are different than they appear to be on the surface. What the three of us never forgot though were all the lessons about life that we learned that day in Caz Park . . .

As we walked down Sage Avenue, Uncle Jim came up with another big surprise for the three of us. As he was walking up the sidewalk to his house he turned back and said, "Guys, I had a real good time today, so thanks fer invitin' me over to yer fishin' spot.

Now I wanna invite all of you ta my favorite spot. I've already talked with yer moms about this, and they all said it'd be okay for me to take the three of you boys down to the Bailey Avenue Yards on the night shift this comin' Friday. What do ya think, boys? Do ya think you'd like ta do that?"

This was really unexpected. "You mean all three of us can go to work with you, Uncle Jim? On the night shift?"

"That's right, Jackie, but just a word a' caution now. Ya' see, I got it all set with the yard master, but only on condition that you boys stay in the control tower while I go out and tend the switches for the trains every so often. Ya see now, this is a real old-fashioned tower, well actually more of a big shanty. The switches are all operated by hand down there, and since we'll be out there durin' the night, it wouldn't be safe for you boys ta be out on the tracks with me, so you'll have to stay inside till mornin' daylight. Now, if that's okay with you . . . Well, whaddya think, guys?"

We all yelled *"SURE!"* together.

"Oh, yeah, one other thing. The shift is twelve ta eight, so we'll take the bus over, but we'll walk back home in the mornin'. It's only about four or five miles, that's all. You can all bring a lunch, and we'll get some breakfast at the Deco Restaurant on the way home. Okay now?"

"Wow! Thanks, Uncle Jim!"

"Yeah, thanks Mister McDonald. Oh boy, this is gonna be *really* neat!"

We were all so excited about going to work on the railroad that we talked about nothing else during the week. I had already answered all sorts of questions about the River Bridge tower, and stirred DJ's and Fisty's imagination with what I had told them. I thought that maybe they were even more excited than I was, if that was possible.

We had to use a transfer ticket from the first bus to the second bus in order to get to the freight yards. It was eleven thirty at night, and this was way past our usual bedtime of ten o'clock. We brought peanut butter sandwiches in a brown bag, and we felt really important, just like grown-ups. We used our imagination while talking about what it would be like to be staying up all night, and being real "railroad men." Uncle Jim just smiled at all of our speculations.

The Bailey Avenue yards were in a huge, flat field about fifty feet down below a long bridge where the cars and buses passed over, high above the tracks. There were only a few small lights in the area so there was total darkness, and it was very hard to see as we walked down the dirt road. Our fear began to build so we stayed close to Uncle Jim. At the bottom of the road we could look up at the bridge, which we had just crossed over in the bus. The lights on the bridge were giving off a dull yellow glow because of the poor quality of lighting technology back then. The strange, dull yellow light conditions gave an eerie look to the bridge and cast long shadows across the railroad yard. The scene was spooky. As we turned towards the main yards at the end of the dirt road we were confronted with an even more spooky sight. There was even less light coming from that direction and what little there was had a more subdued look because it was coming mostly from the dull, yellow-toned headlights of steam engines standing on the tracks in the yard. Dark smoke was curling slowly up from the stacks of several engines, making them appear sinister in the moonlight. Steam was drifting along the ground, sometimes diffusing the small amount of available light. The steady hissing sound of steam could be heard, and every so often the shadow of a railroad worker walking through the clouds of steam in the faint light made everything look mysterious. I don't know about DJ and Fisty, but I could feel my heart pounding as we walked through the darkness towards a tiny shanty at the side of the tracks. Just when we thought our level of fear could be pushed no higher, Uncle Jim said, "Now watch out fer the rats, boys. They're always runnin' around here in the dark because of all the grain mills nearby."

By the time we arrived at the door of the shanty we were just glad to be going anywhere out of that darkness. Although the lighting inside the shanty was the same dull yellow color, the place was kind of cozy, with old-fashioned oak chairs and benches. There was a big oak desk against the far wall where an elderly gray-haired man was hunched over some large train-time sheets. He was writing something on the sheet as he talked to someone on a strange-looking telephone. The phone was attached to the wall by a funny-looking, two-foot-long scissors style arm that extended out from the wall. It looked really old, even for those times. The man was sitting on the same type of chair that I had seen at River Bridge: Large, dark oak, with big wheels and a high, slat-style back. Every time he leaned backwards, the chair would make a squeaking noise that made the place seem even more spooky and mysterious. The glowing potbelly stove in the middle of the room was red hot, and there was a pungent sulfur odor coming from the burning soft coal. The whole atmosphere in that little room made you feel as though you had just traveled fifty years or more back in time.

"Hello there Jimmy me 'buy'. Yer a fine sight fer these old eyes! And how would ye be doin' these days?"

"I'm doin' okay, Paddy. And how about yerself?"

We found out that the gray-haired man was named Paddy Curran, originally from Tipperary, Ireland. He had immigrated to America twenty years before when he was in his forties. His thick Irish brogue accent made it sometimes difficult to understand him, but one thing was for certain: Uncle Jim and Paddy were the best of friends. He had the very light white skin that so many Irish are known for; his cheeks were bright red and his eyes were very light blue. His hair was thick—and pure white. He had a constant smile on his face, and you couldn't help but like the man right away.

"Jimmy, tell me now, is there any news at all on young Joe these days? And how is young Jimmy doin' in the army?" Just about everyone had a relative serving in the military, and people were constantly asking about each other's loved ones.

"No Paddy, I'm sad ta say, nothin' yet. Young Jim is okay, but I'm always worried, 'cause now he's fightin' the "Krauts" in Italy. And by the way, how's yer own boy Johnny doin' these days? I hear he's a naval aviator, is that right?"

"That he is, Jimmy, and he's servin' on one a' those big aircraft carriers somewhere out on the big pond. (The "big pond" was a name for the Pacific Ocean.) He's already shot down three Jap fighters—not bad fer a twenty-three-year-old kid, huh?"

'That sure is somethin' now, Paddy. Say, I want ya ta meet my nephew, Jackie Rossiter, and his buddies, Fisty and DJ. They're gonna be postin' the job with me tonight, Paddy. Oh, by the way, Jackie's dad is Mike Rossiter. You know, the Seneca Street bus driver who went off to fly in the bombers in England."

"Oh, for sure I know yer dad, Jackie, and a fine man he is at that now. Imagine we Irish havin' ta go and rescue those Brits after all they've done ta cause the misery fer our people over so many years. Doesn't that beat all now! Ah, but ya know I just wish they'd get this 'divil' of a war over and done with. War's nothin' but a heartbreaker, that's what it is."

Paddy then turned his attention to Uncle Jim to talk about the change of shift, but before they started with business he wanted to know why Jim was coming out to this "Godforsaken" place, and "on the nightshift ta boot!"

"Jimmy, what in God's name are ye doin' out here in a place like this? What with yer seniority and all ye could have any job ye wish!"

"Well, I wanted ta show these boys the way railroadin' use ta be—before the diesels and all, ya know. I don't think this place is long fer this world, Paddy. Besides, it's also a chance ta see my ol' friend, 'cause maybe the same thing could be said for the likes of two old foggies like us, hey Paddy?" Uncle Jim glanced at me just in time to see the worried look on my face at the thought of his death.

"Course, not fer many years yet, God willin'." Then he winked and smiled at me. It was a reassuring smile that always made me forget whatever was troubling me.

"Say Paddy, how's about playin' yer squeeze box fer me and the boys before ya go home?" Paddy went over to a locker and pulled out a beat-up old concertina. He rolled off a few notes to tune the instrument, and before long we were all singing the words to "Low lie the fields of Athenry." After he finished playing that song he looked over at DJ and said, "I'd be willin' ta bet a few coins that 'DJ' is short fer Daniel Joseph. Am I right son?"

DJ had a look of surprise on his face as he stammered, "Why, how the heck did ya know that, Mister Curran?"

"Well, it's not too hard 'cause Danny sure is one a' the most popular names in all of Ireland, and of course every Irish family has the name Joseph somewhere amongst the boys." With that explanation he broke into the most beautiful of all Irish songs, "Danny Boy."

There we were, in the middle of the night in that desolate, dark place singing Irish songs. We all felt so connected to each other, with the memories of our ancestors' sufferings being awakened with the words of that music. Music has always been such an important part of the Irish past and present. But, soon Paddy had to leave for home.

"Say, Paddy, how will ya be getin' home tonight? I know you've got a long haul out ta the First Ward."

No problem, Jimmy, the boys on job six are gonna drop me off at River Bridge, and I'll be walkin' the rest of the way over ta Smith Street."

"Then you'd best be careful to watch fer those big rats runnin' around down there in the dark, Paddy. Have ya got some clips fer yer trousers? If not yer welcome ta borrow one a' my sets."

Trouser clips were what railroad workers wore when working near the grain mills at night. By clipping your trouser cuffs tight to your ankles it stopped the rats from running up your pant legs in the dark. That's something that had been known to happen, and just the thought of it sent shivers up the back of my neck.

"Thanks anyway, but I'm all set Jimmy. Sorry I gotta leave so soon. Now you and I best be gettin' together more often, old friend. Ye never know when the good Lord will give us the call. Boys, it was a pleasure meetin' and singin' with ye. I know yer in good hands with Jimmy here. God's blessin' on all here—and don't forget now: Keep the faith!" "Keep the faith" was an expression heard often during those trying times. I now realize that the expression was as much about life itself as it was about religion. It was all about not giving up during those days of adversity. In addition to being a form of prayer it was a form of encouragement to each other.

We all said, in unison, "Goodnight, Mister Curran."

After Paddy had left for home, Uncle Jim told us why Paddy had left Ireland to come to America while in the middle years of his life. He sometimes became emotional while telling the story, so we had to wait in silence several times as he paused to reflect. But after ten minutes or so we had the full story, as well as some understanding about that tiny country of our ancestors.

He told us that Paddy had been involved as a young man in the "Easter uprising" of nineteen sixteen and the subsequent battles against the British oppressors of the Catholic people of Ireland. The most hated killers in those days were "The Black and Tans," which referred to the colors of the British special police uniforms. When that term is used, those three words will change the expression on an Irish Catholic's face, because back then every Irish school boy was aware of the cruelty that had been inflicted by the infamous "Black and Tans."

During the civil wars that followed into the nineteen twenties, Paddy's wife and little girl had been caught in crossfire and killed while on their way to a grocery store. In addition, his brother had been imprisoned without trial, and was never heard from again. I asked about his parents.

"His mom passed away in the flu epidemic of nineteen eighteen, and his dad was killed durin' the first uprisin' of nineteen sixteen. Paddy got sick and tired of all the war and killing so he decided ta' come here ta this country with his only remainin' son. And after all those troubles in the past, now his son is off fightin' in this war. God Almighty, sometimes it seems as if our generation just can't get away from the trouble in this world." We sat there quietly as we thought about what he had told us, and Paddy's music continued to play over and over in my mind.

During the night there were all sorts of characters coming into the shanty for one reason or another. Each one had a nickname, as well as stories or jokes to tell. There was "Shorty" Minere, the brakeman, and "Stretch" O'Houllihan, the yard clerk. Then there was "Fats" McCarthy, the Yardmaster, and "Suds" McGillicudy, the "Softheel" (Softheel was the name for a railroad cop). There was Conductor "Ace" McGirk, and "Bones" O'Neill, the "Gandy dancer." Gandy dancer was the name given to the men of the track gangs who had the hardest job of all—laying down the rails and ties. Every one of those characters was good for a laugh, and each one asked if there was any news about Joe, Jim, my dad and the others. Most of them had their own relatives involved in the war somewhere in the world, and there was always mention of offering up a prayer for each other's relatives. This was known as "Sayin' one." (And each man who came into the shanty referred to us boys as "Kid.")

When Bones O'Neill, the Gandy dancer, came into the shanty around five in the morning he wanted to know if Uncle Jim had told us the story about how almost everyone in the yard had gotten drunk on one particular night.

"Now Bones, maybe we shouldn't be tellin' young lads about that kinda stuff. Bad influence ya know!"

"Aw, fiddlesticks Jimmy. It's a fine story, and it teaches a young person how ta be 'resarceful.' *So now, listen here boys. Ya see, one night a carload a' whiskey gets pulled inta the yard—while on its way ta someplace else, ya see. Now every carload a' whiskey has ta have a federal seal on the door—government regulation baloney and all that stuff. Now it's also a rule that the softheels have ta be constantly guardin' the fine contents of such a freight car.*

Well, ya see, these two railroad cops gardin' that wonderful cargo got hungry fer some breakfast, but they couldn't decide which one would go over ta eat first. Then along comes train conductor Paddy Ryan, one a' the finest liars ta ever come out a' Ireland. Well, Paddy convinces the both of 'em that he's an off-duty cop, and he'd be willin' ta spell the both of 'em, if they'd just bring him a cup a' hot coffee.

Those two dopes aren't gone five minutes when the boys in the yard figured out how ta get to the prize without disturbin' that federal seal on the door. Now comes the good part: Ya see, the boys noticed the floor of that car was made out a' wood, then figured that the whiskey inside was bein' shipped in wooden barrels. Well now, don't ya know they just happen ta know where they can find a hand drill with an extra long drill bit. Then right away—up they drill—right through the wooden floor and into the wooden barrel. Next thing ya know everyone's runnin' around the yard lookin' fer containers ta catch the whiskey that's gushin' out under that boxcar!"

By this time, Bones is squealing with delight at the thought of so much free whiskey flowing out from beneath that boxcar. His eyes are twinkling, and his gold fillings are flashing in the yellow light from the potbelly stove as he continues his story.

"Oh gawd now, wouldn't ya know it, we're puttin' whiskey inta everything from dirty coal buckets ta cannin' jars and mop buckets. 'Course, we figered the whiskey would take care a' all those germs. Well now, by the time those dumb softheels get back ta their guard duty, the whole yard crew is already stinko. The first thing the two cops say is: 'Where in the hell is that officer Ryan? He promised ta guard this car fer us!'

"Then I says ta them, 'Officer Ryan?' Oh, you mean that famous Shamus; well he's gone now. He had to go to his own mother's sick bed, poor woman.'

"Well, next thing ya know we're all doubled over with laughter at those two dopes runnin' around that railroad car tryin' ta figger how in the hell we got at that sweet juice without breakin' the seal on the door. Oh gawd, what a sight! I still laugh so hard that I wet myself at the thought of those two morons runnin' around that boxcar in the dark, lookin' fer Paddy Ryan, the 'cop'!"

He paused to catch his breath while we were bent over with laughter at the way he was telling the story as much as what had actually happened.

"So ya see now, boys, next time yer up against a problem, just use a little imagination ta solve the problem. We call that 'common sense', ya' know."

He rattled on with more stories before leaving us laughing about what he referred to as "the big whiskey caper." He offered his final advice before he grinned and closed the door on the way out: *"Remember now boys, whenever yer stuck, and down in the dumps of life, just grab yerselves a drill, aim straight up—and let 'er rip!"*

Soon after that comical man had left, the early light of dawn was beginning to penetrate the darkness. It was just before "quit time," and we were really sleepy after a long night of characters and stories when Uncle Jim sprang another big surprise on us.

"Boys, we won't have to walk as far home as I thought. 'Ace' McGirk is willin' ta give us a lift clear over ta Tifft Farm. That'll put us only a mile er so from home." He paused before smiling and saying, "Of course, we'll have to ride up front on the steam engine with Eddie Hogan, the engineer. That is, if it's okay with you boys?"

Each of us chimed in, "WOW! Okay! Neat! When do we go, Uncle Jim?"

A mixture of fear and excitement surged through us as we climbed up the iron steps of the steam engine. Hogan, the engineer, smiled a wide grin from his position at the throttle. Dempsey, the fireman, otherwise known as "Big Man," opened the large door to the monstrous firebox and began shoveling coal into the already red-hot fire. The locomotive began to rumble down the tracks as we heard the familiar sound of the air brakes releasing—PSSSTT; then the "chug-chug-chug" from the pistons as the wheels began turning and clicking on the rail joints. *The noise became deafening as Big Man kept shoveling the coal into that huge firebox. The fire was so hot that I thought of the devil himself because it sure did look like hell in there.*

It was as if we were on the back of a fire-breathing dragon. The whole contraption was heaving and bending in so many different directions—and all at the same time! There were some parts going in one direction while other parts were moving in the opposite direction. *The monster seemed to be like a mythical giant, creaking with old age, and I could swear that the entire apparatus was actually alive.* Though hard to believe, the deafening noise level continued to build as we gathered speed. Suddenly, Hogan gave a loud blast of the steam whistle, and for just an instant I imagined it to be the roar from that dragon. I looked around at DJ and Fisty, and saw that the look on their faces reflected my own feelings of excitement, fear, joy and wonder. Uncle Jim, Hogan and Big Man were grinning with satisfaction at the effect all of this was having on us boys. *On we chugged, accelerating down the tracks on that sixty-ton monster, streaking through the fields of tall brown grass, speeding past the numerous old industrial buildings.* The three of us were overwhelmed by the experience, and we felt full of power inside of ourselves. By this time our adrenaline valve was wide open.

"WOW!"

Because of the extreme noise and our own fear, we didn't say a single word to each other, but after we climbed down the steps of the engine at Tifft Farm, we made up for it with a steady stream of excited chatter as we walked on home. Uncle Jim just smiled with amusement and satisfaction as we rattled on excitedly about the good time we had on that steam engine. We didn't know it then, but because of our railroad experiences we were about to become celebrities in the neighborhood. When we arrived back home on Sage Avenue, Uncle Jim turned back towards us as he walked up his driveway.

"Be seein' ya' boys. Hope ya' all had a good time!"

Before I could answer, both Fisty and DJ said, *"We SURE did, and thanks a lot,*

Uncle Jim!

Uncle Jim smiled at us, turned and went into his house. When I heard them both say "Uncle Jim," I knew then that something very special had just happened, and it made me feel really good inside.

-CHAPTER FOURTEEN-

BASEBALL GAMES AND ALTAR BOYS

I kept a steady stream of letters going to Dad, telling him about all of the exciting things that we were doing with Uncle Jim. I began to notice a change in the tone of Dad's letters lately. In the following years I would come to realize that his mood was being influenced by all of the death and destruction that was taking place around him on those daily bombing runs. Although he didn't actually say so in his letters, I was slowly learning to "read between the lines" of those letters. I could sense that he was more fearful and saddened by what he was seeing and doing. I would later learn, but only after the war, that he had lost so many of his friends—some while he was a witness to their death in plain sight from his machine gun position. He would tell me to "say a prayer" for Tim and Joe, Pat, Charlie, Stan, Eddie, Johnny, Marty, Harry, and so many other names that I can no longer remember now. He'd never say why they needed our prayers, but he was always emphatic that we were not to forget those names in our intentions.

"Sometimes I feel so tired and lost over here, Jackie. I pray for that day when this war is over and I see all of you again. Take good care of Mom and the girls. Kiss them for me, son. God bless and keep you all safe."

It's a good thing that Uncle Jim was keeping us boys occupied with so many new experiences, because I was slowly becoming more afraid for Dad. The war news was coming at us steadily about fighting in Italy and Russia, and the islands of the South Pacific. There wasn't any news about Joe, and the effect of that was showing on the faces of Aunt Mary and Uncle Joe. There was also the uncertainty about Jim, Phil and Tom, and Gerry Mullaney. Any trouble for either one of them would only add to the grief about the whereabouts and welfare of Joe. This was the constant and corrosive effect of the unknown—no news could be as hurtful as bad news. Not knowing could eat away at you; in the absence of news your imagination would manufacture a fantasy that would only add to your worries. There was just no escape from thinking about the war. Reminders were everywhere: on posters for savings bond drives, on the radio news, and in the movies and daily newspapers. The newsboy could be heard shouting on the street corners, "Read all about it! Jap Kamikazes crash into American ships!" "Roosevelt pledges to step up the pressure!" "Churchill says they'll fight on the beaches!" And, of course, people were constantly asking about each other's loved ones serving "over there," as the saying went. "We'll keep him in our prayers."

Spring returns, and we're starting to play baseball again . . . Trample the grass, find something to make the bases, choose up sides. Take a bat and throw it upright to the other guy. He catches it with one hand, and then you put your hand above his, then his turn, and so on to the end of the bat to determine the winner of first at bat. In the meantime, the pro scouts are watching Mike more than ever. He's almost fifteen now, and getting to be an even better catcher. The scouts are anxious because it'll only be a couple of seasons before they're able to sign him up to a contract. Uncle Jim and the three of us boys go to "Caz" Park together to watch Mike play. Sometimes Father Johnny comes along when he's not busy with his parish duties. I'm bursting with pride and happiness because we're all together, and my "big guy" brother is the talk of South Buffalo. But, there's still a queasy feeling in my stomach because of that stupid war. I wish my dad could be here to enjoy the warm sunny day with us . . . And Jimmy McDonald, and Joe, and Phil, and Tom, and Gerry Mullaney. I say a quick prayer in my mind, and in a flash I wonder if they're ever going to make it home safe again. I'm really scared now, with a sick feeling in my stomach, but my thoughts are brought back to the here and now by the sound of, "PLAY BALL!"

Mike plays to an even higher level this day: He has two doubles and a triple. He picks off a runner at second base; he tags a player out at home even though he's knocked sharply to the ground. As the cloud of dust settles, his hand rises slowly into the air, showing that he still has possession of the ball. "Yer out!" can be heard to the cheers of the partisan crowd. After the game, he comes over to me and says, "Here, Jackie, Dad said to give the next game ball to you." It's a souvenir that I know I'll keep for the rest of my life.

"YER OUT!"

We all walk through the park on our way home to Sage Avenue together. We're constantly hearing, "Hello, and how ya doin'?" from so many of our friends along the way. I'm so proud to be with Mike, my big brother the baseball player, and my cousin, Father Johnny, the parish priest, and of course Uncle Jim, my teacher; and my very best friends, DJ and Fisty. The sun is beginning to set, and for just a while we all forget about the war as we stop at "The Sweet Shop" soda fountain for a cherry coke.

But soon the Wurlitzer "Juke Box" begins playing, and we can hear Jo Stafford, Glenn Miller and Vera Lynne performing the music that is so closely tied into the war. The war is inescapable; it follows you everywhere. There's just no getting away from it. The well-known song, "I'll be seeing you" starts to play. The beautiful words mention a park nearby. Now we can't help it; we're back to talking about our relatives serving so far away from home. We feel so helpless because we can't get right in there and help them with whatever bad situation they may have gotten into. Our frustration and anxiety begins to build. The need to talk about it becomes really strong.

Fisty says, "I wish I was old enough to be over there with Gerry. Boy, I sure do miss him. I hope he's okay." I think to myself how Fisty has always been the tough guy, but the war is starting to eat away at all of us now.

As always, we try to be supportive and keep up a good front, so we try to say something reassuring. "Au sure, Fisty, Gerry's gonna be all right. You'll see!" We all know deep down inside that we're scared as hell for our relatives, but we just can't admit it. We know that at any given minute there's always some enemy soldier trying to kill them, but we want to be tough just like the adults, so we try to cover up our fear. You say to yourself, don't let it show! Only in private do we let our guard down—and then only with our very best friends. It's not about being a "sissy," it's about pulling together and supporting your friends and relatives—we're all a part of the same family.

Father Johnny tries to relieve the tension, so he changes the subject. "Jackie, you're old enough now to take the lessons to become an altar boy. I sure would like to have both you and Mike able to serve the early Mass with me."

He notices my embarrassment in front of the others, so he says quickly, "Of course, there's no big hurry. You can think on it for a while." I smile nervously and mumble something about maybe not being able to learn the Latin. Then I look around cautiously to see if there's any reaction from my two best friends, but I don't see anything unusual.

"Well, like I said, you can just give it some thought for now, Jackie. Hey guys, I gotta get back to work. Had a great time. Heck of a game you played today, Mike."

"Thanks, Father Johnny. See ya at the five thirty on Sunday."'

"Jackie, I'm goin' over ta Milligan's house. See ya at suppertime. So long, guys."

"So long, Mike. What a game! You were really in the sky today!"

"Thanks Fisty. See ya around, guys."

On the way home I'm watching closely for a reaction from Fisty and DJ. I'm worried that they might think I was a sissy for serving Mass because they never did it themselves. I'm anxious to know what they think, so I put out a feeler. "Hey, whadd'ya think, guys? I bet it'd be hard for me ta learn the Latin, huh?"

As always, Fisty takes charge right away. "Nah, I don't think so, Jackie; not with Mike and Johnny ta help ya."

DJ agrees with the assessment, "Sure, Jackie, it'd probably be easy."

They both said "Jackie," so I sensed right away that they thought it would be the natural thing for me to do—not sissy at all. Still, I ventured a little further. "I guess it'd be okay since Mike and Johnny are already doin' it, huh?"

"Sure, why not? What's the matter with you anyway, Jackie?" DJ gives me a quizzical look, and Fisty isn't even paying any attention at all now. It dawns on me that my intuition's all wrong. They must have thought it would be okay to be on the altar with my brother and cousin, even though they had never been altar boys themselves. But, you gotta be careful not to be doin' anything that the group wouldn't like. You NEVER want anyone to think that you're "different."

Sucipiat . . . Dominus . . . Sacrificium. Wow, these words are tongue twisters! As I read through the strange-sounding words I wonder to myself if I'll ever be able to do this. I'm nervous and scared inside when I have to say the prayers in practice session with the other boys. It's after schooltime now, and I'm already tired from classes and the bad dreams about the war the night before. A new parish priest, Father O'Meara, is teaching us our Latin. He's kinda mean, and he seems to enjoy picking on little boys. He smacks a boy on the back of the head, and his eyes light up as he takes delight in the boy's pain.

"All right Rossiter, yer next! Get up here and read the 'Confiteor' . . . and write it out on the blackboard as you say it out loud."

My hand is shaking as I try to write. I'm afraid of Father O'Meara, and I'm embarrassed at the thought of the ten other boys' eyes staring at my back. I miss a word half way through the prayer, and it's then that I feel the priest's hard knee hit my back. Then, as he blows sickening cigar smoke into my face I hear him say:

"Start again, Rossiter!"

My stomach begins to feel queasy from the cigar smoke, but somehow I get through the prayer without making another mistake. I feel extreme relief from the tension when I hear him say:

"Okay Rossiter, sit down. Talty, yer next. Get on up here!"

As the same routine is played out on the ten other boys, my body goes limp. I'm mentally and physically exhausted. I slump down in my seat without being aware of it. Then suddenly, I'm jolted sharply out of my day dreaming by Father O'Meara's loud voice.

"Rossiter! Sit up straight! Pay attention or you'll be up here again, boy!"

"Yes, Father O'Meara. Yes, sir!"

Oh God, this is awful. Why did I ever get involved with this? It's no wonder DJ and Fisty didn't want any part of this stuff!

To this day I still can't figure out how I ever became qualified to serve Mass. Maybe it was because I'd be serving with Mike, and he could keep an eye on me while I was on probation. Now the clothes of an "altar boy" were something called a cassock and surplice. They were bright red and white, and when I was dressed that way I looked very innocent and holy. Sometimes, when I couldn't remember the prayer I'd put my head down and mumble in a real low voice. Father Johnny would correct me gently, but when I had to serve for Father O'Meara I couldn't make any mistakes or I'd get the cigar smoke treatment again. "You'll regret it if you ever give me that mumble routine again, Rossiter!"

There were times when I wanted to tell Father Johnny about

Father O'Meara, but I didn't want to be labeled a sissy. There were so many times when we carried these worries around with us in those days. I guess we used our playtime to help us relax some. Nowadays, during these times, the pressures of daily life are so much more complex for kids. I often wonder how the young people find a way to deal with the increased pressures that they surely must face.

After several months of serving Mass, an amusing incident occurred that showed the other side of Father O'Meara's personality. One evening, there was an old and senile Monsignor from another parish preaching on and on about murder! He kept droning away, and no one could understand his point. It was hot in the sacristy (that's the priest's dressing room), and we were all growing tired while the droning continued on, seemingly without end. We were uncomfortable sitting there sweating in our heavy vestments. I guess Father O'Meara couldn't stand it any longer because he suddenly blurted out, "If he doesn't get off the altar real soon, murder just might be committed right here and now!"

Well, Mike and I started the giggles—something that would normally infuriate any one of the priests, but Father O'Meara said not one word of admonishment to either one of us. We knew that was because our defense would be that it was his remark that started it in the first place. We never mentioned the incident to anyone else since we also knew what would happen to us if we did.

The hardest part of my new job was getting up at five o'clock on Sunday mornings for the five thirty Mass. The first time that I served with Mike and Father Johnny turned out to be quite an experience, because when we came out on the altar to start the Mass, the church was really crowded—especially for that time of the day. Not only was everyone from the three families in the church that day, but also most of the neighbors from Sage Avenue were there. I guess people wanted to see all three Rossiters together on the altar for the first time. It made me feel like some sort of a celebrity. The biggest surprise was when I saw Fisty and DJ right up front in the first pew. I couldn't believe it, and even though I was sleepy I became really nervous. I did feel proud though—

especially when my buddies grinned and gave me the thumbs-up signal. I was also glad that they didn't think I was a sissy in those funny-lookin' clothes.

On the way home we all stopped at Miller's bakery for hot cross buns before heading home for breakfast. That was the morning of June four, nineteen forty-four. Two days later we'd hear the news about the most important day of the war. We had absolutely no idea that some of our worst fears were about to be realized. Heartache was just forty-eight hours away.

-CHAPTER FIFTEEN-

THE ANGUISH OF D-DAY

On Monday, June fifth, I was notified that I was hired to deliver the afternoon newspaper! My route would be on our street, and two other streets close by. I'd be delivering one hundred and eighty-three papers, six days per week. I was to receive one quarter of a cent for each paper delivered. I got my pencil and spiral notebook from school out, and found that I would be earning almost two dollars and seventy-five cents a week! The news company was going to give me the use of a wagon to deliver the papers, but I'd have to pay twenty-five cents per week for the next twenty weeks until the five dollars cost was paid off. But that would still leave me with two dollars and fifty cents a week to help out at home. Oh boy, did I ever feel important at the thought of being able to help out at home! Besides, Margaret, Maureen and Mike were already helping out with their own part-time jobs. However, my excitement about the amount of money would eventually be tempered some when I found out how hard it was to collect all of the money owed every week. But, at least for now the world seemed like a beautiful place to me. I was gonna earn a paycheck!

On Wednesday afternoon I was on my way home after making my deliveries, and as I approached Uncle Jim's house I spotted several of my relatives, including Mom, out on his front porch. I got scared right away when I saw that everyone was crying. I felt a strong surge of fear come over me because my first thought was that something had happened to Uncle Jim. My mind and body seemed to just freeze in place. "Jackie, something terrible happened. Jimmy McDonald was killed in France yesterday. The telegram just came a while ago." For just an instant I felt guilty because I was relieved that it wasn't Uncle Jim. But then the reality of how much this would hurt my uncle replaced my feelings of guilt.

"Where's Uncle Jim now, Mom?"

"He's on his way home from work. He doesn't know it yet, Jackie."

We all sat there in silence for about thirty minutes, each one of us alone with our personal grief, waiting for that good man to come around the corner from Seneca Street on his walk home from work. By the time he rounded the corner with his lunch bucket tucked under his arm, the number of people had grown to a large group because the neighbors had been coming over steadily. He paused for several seconds, and just stared from about a hundred feet away when he saw so many people in front of his house. He put his head down and walked slowly towards us. I could tell right away that he knew something bad had happened. When he came closer we could see the tears already running down his cheeks . . . He seemed to know without being told what the news was. As I watched him, I learned for the very first time that day the meaning of the word "heartbroken."

He stared into Aunt Mary's eyes and said, "What's the category of the telegram, Mary . . . wounded?" There was an air of hopefulness in his voice as he said, "wounded?"

Her voice cracked as she hugged him and said, "No, Jim . . . he's gone."

He cried out, "Oh, my God!" Then he buried his face into her shoulder.

We all started crying as we crowded in around him in a circle, as if trying just a bit too late to protect him from the outside world. That day was one of the saddest days of my young life.

There was just a memorial Mass at Saint Bridget's because Jimmy would be buried in France, very close to where he had been killed on Omaha Beach. Later on we found out that a permanent cemetery was to be located in a field on a high bluff overlooking those same beaches where such a high price had been paid to free the people of France from Nazi rule. Not surprisingly, the church was overflowing with people that day. I could see quite a few military uniforms in the crowd of people, some young men home on leave, and some with injuries that weren't visible. But there were several others that I saw who had missing arms and legs. Many of those boys were life-long friends of Jimmy and his dad. We were back to calling him "Jimmy" again now that he was gone. We wanted to remember him always as our dear young friend when he was just one of the boys in the neighborhood—before that war came and took him away from us. Uncle Jim insisted that DJ, Fisty and myself sit next to him in the front pew. His eyes were bloodshot from what he was going through, but he was able to smile gently as he said to us, "Now you boys stay real close ta me, would ya?"

"We sure will, Uncle Jim."

"Are you okay, Uncle Jim?"

"As long as yer here with me, I am, boys. As long as yer here with me . . . . Boys, do ya see that tall man sitting over there behind us, the one in the dark blue suit?"

"Yeah, we do Uncle Jim. Who is that man, Uncle Jim? Do we know him?"

Yes, you do, boys. That's Jack O'Shea from the railroad."

Jack O'Shea nodded to us, but he had a difficult time as he attempted to put a smile on his face. There were just too many tears running down his cheeks, and so he just put his head down and looked away.

Father Johnny and Monsignor Foley were so emotionally shaken that they asked Father O'Meara to speak at the Mass. O'Meara was very new to the priesthood himself, about the same age as Johnny. He had grown up in a small town about fifty miles away, and he was still just catching on about the people of our parish. He must have grasped the situation that day, because he did a surprisingly good job when he spoke. In fact, we all noticed that there was a big change in him after that day, and it was for the better.

"Mister McDonald, Maureen, Kathy, relatives and friends. Your loss is so terrible: an only son, an only brother, and a dear friend to so many people. This crowded church is a testament to so many close friends of the McDonald family. For me, today, this service for young Jimmy becomes very personal for myself and my own family back home. You see, Vincent O'Meara, my younger brother, was killed in action last year out there in the Pacific war. It seems that no matter where you go today you find so many families who have suffered a terrible loss such as ours because of this war. So many young people have been taken from us before they could enjoy their youth. Mister McDonald, before this service began I had an opportunity to talk to some of your friends and relatives that have come here today to honor your son's memory.

"I spoke to your neighbors from Sage Avenue, the neighborhood in general, and of course your many fellow employees who are here from the railroad. The message coming through constantly was that young Jimmy was so very much like his dad—a fine person. I'm certain that there was more than just that respect as the measure of young Jimmy's life, but if that respect was the only result of his twenty years here on earth, then you, Mister McDonald, have done your duty well as a father. And now young Jimmy is, like my own brother, in the hands of God.

"May you his father, his sisters, his cousins and friends be comforted throughout your own life with the many good memories of this fine young man. May God's blessing be upon each and everyone here at this Mass. And finally, let's all pray to God to protect Jimmy's relatives and friends—and all the other young men who are continuing the fight against the enemy even as we speak here today. May the peace of our Lord be with them and yourselves during these terrible and dark days of heartache."

> Dear Dad
>
>   I guess Mom already told you about Jimmy. Me and Fisty and DJ are gonna stay real close to Uncle Jim during the summer. We've been sittin' with him on his front porch a lot. We talk about lots of things. He's been tellin' us stories about when he was in the First World War. Some of the stories are real funny, but sometimes he gets sad too.

He told us about someplace called Saint Miheil in France where he was in a big battle with the Germans, and lots of his friends died there. When he talked about all his friends bein' buried there in the cemetery he had tears in his eyes. Everybody stops by to talk to him and try to cheer him up 'cause he's really lonely now.

Well, anyway, I don't have to go to Children's Hospital very much anymore. Now it's every three months, but I gotta see Doc Carden in between the visits. They said they got it under control now, but they warned me about hoppin' garages and hitchin' cars, and climbin' trees. They said no more a' that stuff. I still have to take one pill everyday, and drink lots of water.

Mike is playin' really good baseball now. He gets better everyday. We all go to watch him play at Caz Park. Those men from New York and Cleveland still come to watch him play. They said to say hello to you. I'm pretty busy lately, 'cause now I'm an altar boy, plus I got a job deliverin' the newspaper. I make only about two dollars a week 'cause some people pretend they already paid me, but they didn't.

We heard that Tom and Phil didn't go to the big invasion at Normandy, but Father Johnny says they're both fightin' the Germans now in Southern France. So far they're both okay, at least I guess so. Mom is still workin' hard with Uncle Joe and Mrs. Corrigan. All the girls are okay too. We all miss you, Dad. We always worry about you and our cousins Joe, and Phil and Tom. Fisty worries about his brother Gerry in the Marines. It seems like everybody is gone away to fight in the war. We wish the war would just go away so everyone could come home again.

I been pretty busy lately with bein' an altar boy and deliverin' the newspapers. Mom said she told you all about it. The whole church was full when they had the Mass for Jimmy. Mike served Mass, but I didn't 'cause Uncle Jim wanted me to sit with him. Margaret, Maureen and Mary are doin' okay. Margaret and Maureen are doin' odd jobs to help out at home. Mike is workin' at the Sweet Shop now, and his pay helps out at home too. We all want to help Mom save up to buy our own house someday. We hope you can come home real soon, Dad. We miss you a lot.

Love, Jackie

During that summer the four of us spent more and more time together fishing at Caz Creek, workin' on the railroad, and just sittin' around and talkin' for hours on Uncle Jim's front porch. Our time spent together was fulfilling a need for all of us. DJ's dad had passed away, Fisty's dad was usually down at Murphy's bar, and my dad was in England. A lot of what we knew later on in life as men we learned from Uncle Jim during that summer of nineteen forty-four. By the time school reopened in September, our friendship with him had been forged for the rest of our lives. We would sit out on his front porch for hours—sometimes well past dark while he told us stories about his youth.

"Yeah boys, I was a crazy kid sometimes. I even had an old motorcycle I use ta drive up and down the dirt roads out in the country." He started to chuckle to himself.

"I use ta like drivin' through the farm pastures, and one time this ol' bull gets real mad and he starts chasin' me round and round through all the manure. Well, next thing ya know this ol' farmer comes out a' the barn with a double barrel shotgun blazin'. It's a good thing his aim was bad, but I got scared and went slidin' inta the manure pile. He was still reloadin' as I took off down the road or I might not even be here ta tell about it! Boys, it took about three days ta get the stink off me."

"Tell us about when you were in the army, Uncle Jim."

"Well Fisty, there was this time when me and my Canadian pal were ordered ta guard this bank in Alsace, France. Well, actually there wasn't much left ta guard, 'cause all the walls were blown apart. The only thing left standin' was this big safe right in the middle of all that damage. Now this captain says that we're not ta let anybody near that safe. He says, "That's an order, soldiers!"

"Well, a couple a' days go by and the captain's still not comin' back ta tell us what ta do. Then about that time a couple of old French guys stop by and give me and my buddy a bottle of somethin' called Pernod, some kinda strong French drink. There we are drinkin' away and feelin' pretty good from this Pernod stuff when we hear that the captain's been killed in an accident. By this time we're really stoned good on that French booze, and my buddy gets this idea. He says we could put all our grenades on the door a' that safe and blow it open. Next thing ya know, BAM! And the door falls right off!"

By this time he's grinning at the memory of his story, and were glad that he's got his mind off of his grief, even if it's only for a while.

"Ya know boys, that Canadian friend a' mine, he must have known that those bonds were valuable 'cause he's pretty rich these days. We been keepin' in touch all these years. He even sent me this expensive watch just last week."

"Wow, Uncle Jim, that's really nice lookin'!"

"Yeah it is nice. Ya see I took six watches from that safe, and I gave five of them away ta my other buddies, but I lost the one I kept fer myself. So my Canadian pal says he wanted ta replace my lost watch. Pretty nice a' him after all these years."

He had a far off quizzical look on his face, and then he said, "Ya know I think he said those bonds were 'negotiable securities'— or somethin' like that. Yeah, a real smart guy . . . "

Of course at that age young boys will always revert to the pastimes that interest young boys. We played baseball in the field, went fishing at the "Old Log" and then started to do something new down at the field. It was Fisty's idea, and DJ and I thought it was a really good idea.

"Let's start campin' out overnight in the field. We could build a fire and set up a lean-to. I know a guy named Jimmy Finnegan who's in the Boy Scouts. He says he'll show us how ta set it up."

"Wow, Fisty. That sounds great, but we gotta get our moms ta give us the okay."

"Ah sure, but we can just sweet talk 'em with the malarkey. You know how they think we're all little angels, right Jackie?"

DJ and I started warmin' up to the idea. DJ said, "Hey, we can bring some cans of that Dinty Moore Beef Stew!"

"Yeah, and maybe some wieners ta cook over the fire too."

"Oh, by the way you guys, there's only one problem. Jimmy Finnegan's really ugly."

"Ah so what? Not everybody can be as pretty as you, Fisty!"

"No DJ, I mean REALLY ugly. In fact, they call him "Pusshead" Finnegan 'cause he's got so many big pimples on his face and neck. Well, anyway, you'll see what I mean."

Boy, oh boy, Fisty wasn't kiddin'. That guy was one of the most ugly guys I ever saw. His head was kind of oversized, and it was full of hundreds of pimples of every shape, size and description. He wore thick horned rim glasses that had a big wad of white medical tape holding them together on the bridge of his nose. Not only was his nose extra large, but it was also twisted like a corkscrew! His oversized ears made him look like an elephant—or maybe one of the seven dwarfs. His glasses were as thick as the bottom of a Coke bottle, making his eyes seem even bigger than they already were. They looked like they were gonna bulge right out of their sockets. He showed a bunch of oversized brown teeth every time he smiled. He said he hated to waste time combing his hair, so it always looked like a bird's nest. But, strangely enough we kinda liked this guy right away. Maybe it was because we felt sorry for him, I don't know. There was just somethin' about his attitude that you had to admire. He had no illusions—he understood fully that he was ugly, but he kind of brushed it aside, ignored it, and just went ahead doing his own thing. I guess he had learned to accept it as part of his life. To the three of us this gave him kind of an endearing quality, and one thing was for sure: This guy wasn't a phony. Besides, he offered to pay for all the Dinty Moore Beef Stew and even some bottles of pop!

Well, at any rate, we decided to try not to use his nickname even though he said he'd gotten used to it, and he didn't give a damn anymore. He really knew a lot about campin' out, and he showed us how to do all the things we had to know about to "survive out in the wild." On the first night out in the lean-to we didn't want to admit how afraid we were. The conversation went something like this:

"What was that?" "What was what?" "That noise." "I didn't hear any noise." "Well, hell on you, there's somethin' out there!" "Why don't you go check it out?" "Screw you, no way!" "Well I'm not goin' out there alone!" "Why not, are ya chicken?" Oh, oh, there's that chicken word. "I'll fix yer butt in the mornin'" "What about right now, or are you chicken?"

The noise was usually something like a raccoon, but we'd stay awake most of the night wondering. We'd pass the night by telling ghost stories, then we'd hear another noise and the chicken debate would start all over again. We were always tired by the time the sun came up. We got to love campin' out in the field, so we went out at least one night almost every week of the summer. We were havin' a great time until that day in late summer when things started to "heat up" fast.

In August, Uncle Jim received a letter from Jimmy's company commander. Dad's Uncle Joe read the letter to everyone at his house one evening. His voice cracked several times, and we were all in tears—even Fisty and DJ. That was one of the few times that I can recall when it was okay to show your emotions. It's not that anyone said that it was okay, but there were a few times like that evening when you just knew instinctively that it was okay.

> Dear Master Sergeant McDonald,
>
>   I'm writing this letter to you about one of the finest young soldiers I ever had the privilege to know—your son, Jimmy. Lance Corporal McDonald was a real man, one who cared as much for his fellow soldiers as he did for himself.
>
>   Believe it or not he was always looking out for the "younger" guys—the eighteen—and nineteen-year olds. Jimmy was dragging the wounded body of an eighteen-year-old buddy towards some cover on Omaha Beach when he was killed instantly by gunfire coming from the cliffs above the beach. Unfortunately, his buddy, Private Tom Brady of Boston Massachusetts was also hit by the same gunfire and died.
>
>   Just a few minutes before trying to save his friend he

had remained out in the open on the beach while providing covering fire with his automatic weapon. This action helped countless numbers of his company, as well as others, to find shelter from the heavy machine gun fire that was raking the beach. I'm absolutely certain that his action saved many lives that awful day on the beach. Because of that heroic and selfless action on the part of your son, I have recommended him for the Silver Star for gallantry in action.

Your son's body, as well as the body of Tom Brady, has been buried in a temporary cemetery not far from the beach where all of this took place. It's my understanding that in time a permanent cemetery will be constructed just above that beach where Jimmy and so many other young men died while helping to win freedom for the people of France.

Mister McDonald, on a personal note, I hope you don't mind my using your previous U.S. Army rank at the beginning of this letter. You see, Jimmy spoke proudly of what you had done in your lifetime. We had many conversations while we were fighting in the Italian campaign, and through Jim I feel as though I got to know you. For that reason it is so much more difficult for me to write to you, sir.

I'll never forget your son, Mister McDonald. I can only hope that someday my ten-year-old son becomes as good a man as Jimmy was. May God watch over you and keep you well, Master Sergeant McDonald.

Respectfully,
Captain Matthew Anderson

Before long everyone on the street, and then the whole neighborhood heard about the Silver Star award. My buddies and me talked a lot about it, but we noticed that Uncle Jim became more quiet and thoughtful after that letter came, so we stopped talking about it around him. We just didn't want to do anything at all to hurt his feelings.

-CHAPTER SIXTEEN-

JACKIE ROSSITER GETS
"WOUNDED IN ACTION"

While down at our "fort" in the field one day in July we became bored, and when DJ came up with an idea for a "rock war" down near the river, we're all in agreement that it would be a fun thing to do. A rock war is pretty basic stuff, and it's as close to a duel as you can come without being killed. Of course at our age we didn't really think that we could ever be killed—why heck, we just knew that we were gonna live forever.

The rules were simple: We go down to the stone island near the river where there are plenty of fist-sized rocks that have been polished smooth by the thousands of years of flowing water. Next, you stand about one hundred feet away from each other. One person gets first throw at his opponent, and then the other guy gets his turn. Odd-even fingers from behind the back determine who will be first to throw at his opponent. Now theoretically the other person sees the rock coming in time to duck out of the way. Of course we had no understanding whatsoever of the meaning of a big word like theory—we actually thought that you could duck out of the way. Heck, we'd seen Flash Gordon do it plenty of times at The Orpheum. After deciding that Fisty and I would be opponents, and that DJ and "Pusshead" Finnegan would be opponents, we squared off with the finest, smoothest rocks we could find. Keep in mind that at that age we just weren't very bright. Well, actually, now that I think about it we were just plain stupid I guess.

DJ gets to throw at Pusshead first. Oh, oh, the stone finds its mark on Finnegan's thigh. "Owww! That hurt! You did that on purpose, DJ!"

"Well look, dummy, yer supposed ta duck out a' the way, ya know!"

"You guys didn't tell me that!"

"You mean you gotta be told?"

Next, "Pusshead" gets his turn to throw at DJ, but DJ's quick as a cat and the stone misses its mark.

"Hey, DJ, that's not fair. You jumped out a' the way."

"So what? You think I'm stupid enough to just stand there?"

"Well, I did."

"That's yer problem. Now start duckin' 'cause I wouldn't wanna damage yer pretty face, Jimmy!"

Now it's Fisty's turn to use me as a target, and I'm still laughin' at the remark about Pusshead's "pretty face." Wow, IMPACT right on the top of the forehead! Stars start shooting in front of my eyes, the world starts spinning, and then all the lights go out. I'm vaguely aware of someone talking off and on.

"Holy God, Fisty—you killed him!"

"Oh shut up, 'Pusshead.' He ain't dead. *At least I don't think so anyway."*

"Yeah but he's really bleedin' good. Maybe we should put a tourniquet on it. I saw that in the movies once."

"Oh yeah, well where we supposed ta put it? On his neck, ya dope!"

I hear them all laughing. What the hell are they laughin' about? I thought I was their friend? The world starts spinning again. Everything goes as black as the spooky coal bin.

Fisty tries to reassure me. "Hold still, Jackie. I got my under shirt tied around yer forehead. It's really bleedin' good!"

A bright light causes me to blink and squint. *It's the sun! I'm still alive!*

"Hey, I remember now, what the heck were you guys laughin' about? Oh boy, am I ever dizzy!"

"Lay back down fer a minute, Jackie. Don't worry, we'll get ya home."

My new white sweatshirt's now half-red from all the blood, even though Fisty's white tee shirt has absorbed most of the blood. Seeing all that blood starts to scare the hell out of me, but Pusshead says, "Yer head bleeds a lot when it's cut." Says he learned that in the Scouts.

All that I could think was, *Oh my God, what's my mom gonna say now.*

As we walk down Sage Avenue, the neighbors are all running out to ask what happened? Fisty's now afraid that he's gonna get in trouble, so he concocts a story that will eventually make me out to be a big hero in the neighborhood. Of course, at that time with the blood still gushing out of my forehead I'm just not interested in his explanation about what happened.

"Oh my God, Jackie, what happened to you?" Mom's eyes are full of fear and panic as she rushes me into the house to get some ice for the gash on my forehead. I can't answer the long list of question that she's posing because my head is throbbing with pain. The room starts to spin, and off I go into that world of distorted reality again. Then the lights go out, and I'm once more back in that spooky coal bin in the cellar.

When the lights come on again several hours later I find myself in a hospital bed. The first thing I see is Mom sitting there with the same look of fear that I had seen in the kitchen at home.

"Jackie, oh thank God you're all right. We've all been so worried about you. How are you feeling? Can I get you something? Is there anything that you want?"

She's so distraught that she's asking more questions than I can answer. I answer with my own question. "How long do I have to stay here, Mom? I wanna go home, okay?"

"Doctor Cardin says that you had a concussion so you'll have to stay for a couple of days. They used fourteen stitches to close that cut on your head. That's why it's bandaged. Jackie, you know I told you to stop antagonizing those Polish boys across the river. I can't understand why you boys want to fight with them all the time."

"Huh? Whaddya mean, Ma?"

"You know darn well what I mean, Jackie. The Mullaney boy said that this happened because of a fight with the Polish boys from across the river."

"Oh yeah, I guess I forgot, Ma."

"Say, Jackie, what's wrong with that Finnegan boy? His face looks awful. Was he in an accident of some kind?"

"No Mom, I guess he was just born that way."

"Oh, what a shame. I'll say some prayers for him!"

That generation looked upon prayer as the most powerful medicine around. Medical technology back then was in the Stone Age compared to today, and there was a strong reliance on prayer as the final answer to all problems. Of course, I've known some pretty tough guys over the years that would fall back on prayer when they were faced with a serious illness. But, at that age we didn't want to be called a "sissy," so we just pretended that we didn't hear some things.

Now I wondered what the heck kinda story has Fisty been spreadin' around the neighborhood? When they let me go home a few days later I found out that Fisty had dreamed up a good one, so nobody would blame him for what happened to me. I had to admit that it was a pretty creative story, and I sure did enjoy bein' a hero in the neighborhood.

"Well, Jackie, ya see I told everybody that the Polacks did that to you when they were attackin' our side of the river. I said we held them off even though they outnumbered us, and had BB guns and rocks. Everyone thinks we're heroes now, even Pusshead . . . er, I mean Jimmy Finnegan. They think yer the biggest hero 'cause you got wounded in action!" His eyes lit up because he was off the hook and we were now celebrities.

"Darned good story, Fisty!"

"I figgered you'd like it! Pretty good malarkey, huh, Jackie boy?"

After a few weeks I got to feelin' kinda guilty because everybody believed that I was some sort of hero. To me the only real heroes in the world were guys like my dad, over there on the other side of the world fighting to save mankind. They were the ones who were taking all the risks. Then there were people like my uncle Jim protecting kids like us at home. Every time I thought of that day when the Polish big guys chased us down the street I remembered how afraid I had been. At that time of my life I figured that real heroes weren't afraid of anything, and it made me feel guilty to be called a hero. I couldn't live with the lie any longer so I told the truth in the neighborhood about what happened that day. That's when I found that a fallen hero could be a painful experience too, because of the "squealer" label. Fisty and the guys got mad at me for about oh, two days, I think. When I explained how I felt about who the real heroes were they had to agree that those were the only people who deserved a hero label. For a while we were laughed at for being impostors, but before long we just forgot about it because something more exciting was already tempting us. That was about the time we started diving off the top of the railroad bridge into the river just like we had seen the big guys doin'.

-CHAPTER SEVENTEEN-

FACE TO FACE WITH DEATH

The danger involved in divin' off the top of the railroad bridge ranked right up there with hitchin' cars and rock wars. As we all grew older we found it hard to believe that we hadn't killed ourselves when we were so young, had so little fear . . . and so few brains.

The railroad bridge was in between Kaisertown and South "Bufflo." I'd estimate that the top girders were about thirty feet above the water. The water was about twenty feet deep at that point—and pretty dirty from the industrial pollution in the area. But the most fascinating attraction was the abandoned boxcar lying upright on the bottom of the river beneath the bridge. The rail car reportedly had derailed off the tracks a few years before and had been left down there in the water. Since the doors were open on each side, a diver could swim down, go through one doorway and then out the other before coming back up to the surface. We were about to get ourselves into trouble again.

Naturally, Fisty always took charge, so he was the first to try it.

"Hey, that's neat down there! A little spooky 'cause it's kinda dark, especially when yer inside the boxcar, but it's a blast!"

He was right, it sure was scary on the first try, but it wasn't so bad after you got used to it. There wasn't much room for error on how long it took though, because I was just about out of breath by the time I got back up to the surface. One thing was certain: Pusshead Finnegan was even more ugly with all of his clothes off—if that's possible! Come to think of it, we must have all looked pretty funny up on top of that bridge without a stitch on. Yep, there we were, the four of us way up on top of that bridge, thirty feet above the water and completely in the nude when along comes some Polish girls! They were really enjoying our embarrassment until they got a good close-up look at Pusshead Finnegan. That scared the hell out of 'em and they took off. They could still hear us laughing after them as they ran screaming through the field towards Kaisertown. Right about that time we noticed that Pusshead had been diving into the water several times, but he still had his coke bottle glasses on. We were amazed that he hadn't lost them. Like DJ said, "Maybe they're stuck to his pimples!"

Diving off that bridge was exciting fun, but it all came to an end a few weeks later when I got the biggest scare of my young life. After we took our clothes off we did odd-even fingers to see who was gonna dive first. I won, but for many years afterwards I wished that I had never gone first that day. Anyway, I knifed into the water and started down towards the open door. It was a cloudy day so it was a little darker down there than usual. I swam slowly through the first door, and then I suddenly came face to face with the dead body of another boy! I'll never forget the stare of his open eyes as his body was floating against the roof of the boxcar. His arms were outstretched as though he was a skydiver, and he was facing me, in reverse of how we normally entered the boxcar. I turned around to swim back out as fast as I could. I was in full panic now and able to swim a lot faster than normal. Just as I was coming to the surface, Fisty dove into the water in between the boxcar and me. The usual practice was that we waited for the first diver to clear, but Fisty was in a hurry that day. He hadn't seen me come back up because he hit the surface of the water just as I was breaking the surface on the way up.

What followed next was a comedy of errors, because as I had just finished yelling to Pusshead and DJ what I had seen, Fisty came back up above the surface. He was shouting and crying at the same time as he blurted out, "Jesus Christ Almighty, Jackie's down there! I think he's dead in the boxcar!"

Just then he saw me, and thought that I had been pulling a joke on him because he started yelling at me, "You craphead! What are you doin' tryin' ta scare the hell out a' me like that for? Damn you, that's not funny, Jackie!" His face was bright red with fear and anger.

"I wasn't tryin' ta fool you, Fisty. That wasn't me down there; it was someone else. I don't know who it is. I was really scared too! That's why I came back up!"

Fisty always had to be the strong, silent type, so he was embarrassed at showing so much emotion, and he was mad as hell because he thought I had pulled a sick joke on him. But I realized in the flash of that stressful moment just how much Fisty valued my friendship, and that gave me a good feeling that stayed with me for the rest of my life. Of course, I felt the same way about him too.

Fisty dove back down and pulled the boy's lifeless body up to the surface, and over to the shore. When we turned the body upright I recognized the face of Joey Sweeney, one of my fellow altar boys! "What's the matter, Jackie? You look like ya just saw a ghost. Do you know this kid?"

I answered in a low, subdued voice, "Yeah, he's Joey Sweeney from Cumberland Street. He's an altar boy, too." My heart was pounding like a drum.

We didn't know a thing about how to try to revive the boy, but it wouldn't have mattered anyway. His face and neck had turned dark purple; he wasn't breathing and he didn't have a pulse. His body was already kinda stiff. We figured he'd been in that boxcar for quite a while. None of us had ever seen a dead boy before, especially up close like that. The only dead people we had ever seen were at funeral homes, and they were all fixed up to look good.

We had all been silent for several moments, and I felt a need to say something, anything. "What are we gonna do?"

Jimmy Finnegan said, "We better call the cops right away!"

Fisty said, "I don't know about that, Jimmy. We could get into big trouble 'cause maybe the cops would start thinkin' we had somethin' ta do with it. Besides, we'd probably get inta trouble fer divin' off the bridge too, ya know."

The four of us debated over and over again about what we

should do. We were too young, too inexperienced, and too afraid that somehow we'd be accused of doing something bad. We worried about all of the possible trouble that we could get into just by having been there at the wrong time. Finally, we decided to get dressed and go over to O'Malley's drug store where we would make an anonymous phone call to police station number nine. Before leaving the river we lodged Joey's body onto the riverbank. On the way over to O'Malley's we swore a sacred oath to each other that we would never squeal about this to anyone, ever. We also vowed that we'd never go back to the railroad bridge again. The first vow caused us years of anguish. We all had the biggest scare of our young lives, and I knew that each one of us was shaken badly by that day. I don't know if the others had nightmares, but I had lots of them. I never mentioned the bad dreams to the other guys because I was always worried about the "chicken" label. Besides, we all knew without saying so that all of us had those bad dreams. Keeping a secret like that is really stressful when you're just a young kid.

What made it all the more difficult for the four of us was that the death of Joey Sweeney was the number one topic of conversation in the neighborhood for months afterwards. It was an exceptional event because things like that hardly ever happened. Whenever we thought about people dying, especially a young person, it was always in connection with the war. All four of us boys heard the questions and lectures from our parents.

"Jackie, did you know that Sweeney boy who died down there near that river?"

"Yeah, Mom, but we weren't good friends. I just knew him from the altar boy classes, that's all." I could feel the skin on my face begin to heat up because of the secret that I was carrying around with me.

"If you didn't know him then why is your face turning red, Jackie? Are you sure you don't know anything about what happened?" Oh, oh. She suspects something. Think fast, Jackie!

"Oh, it's just that I get real scared when I hear anything about it, Mom." Lying, especially to her, was always very difficult for me.

She said that my eyes gave away my secret, and I just knew that she was trying to see what my eyes were telling her now.

"Well, I don't want you to go anywhere near that river anymore. You know, all the people on the street said that he might have been divin' off that bridge. Now you promise me that you'll never go near that river again, okay?"

"I swear to God, Mom. I'll never go near the river again."

"Okay then, go ahead and play outside now." Staying away from the river was another vow that would be easy to keep—for the four of us.

-CHAPTER EIGHTEEN-

A HOT TIME DOWN IN THE FIELD

It seemed as though there was never a dull moment that summer. There was always something to do, and we were always good at getting ourselves into trouble. We looked forward to spending time with Uncle Jim. Sometimes it was going to work on the railroad with him (now it was all four of us boys), or just sitting on his front porch while he gave us the benefit of the wisdom he had gained during his life. And then there were the fishing trips to "The Old Log," and watching Mike play baseball at Caz Park. There was also that brief interlude of a couple of weeks when we were diving off the bridge. Since we wanted to forget all about that incident we stepped up our camping out in the field. But, as usual, trouble was always just around the corner waitin' for us.

One day Jimmy Finnegan brought one of his mother's frying pans down to the field. "Now look, you guys, it's okay ta use it but ya gotta take good care of it, 'cause it's my mom's very best fryin' pan!"

He seemed to be obsessed with that frying pan, but it looked like any other frying pan to us. It was the typical frying pan of those times: plain, black, heavy cast iron. It was nice and big so we were able to put lots of food in it to cook for the four of us. We thought that it was pretty funny 'cause he was so nervous about that dumb frying pan. Every time we finished eating, Pusshead would tell us: "Hey you guys, don't forget to wash the fryin' pan real good! It's my mother's very best fryin' pan, ya know!"

While walking through the field towards home one day we decided to stop and have a "smoke." Fisty had stolen a Lucky Strike cigarette from his father's pack, and we were passing it around and takin' drags on it. This was something new to us, especially DJ and me, so he and I start getting a queasy feeling in our stomach. DJ and I steal knowing glances at each other, but we we're afraid to say anything because we didn't want to be called sissies, a term that described anyone afraid to try something new. We pretended that we enjoyed the smoking.

DJ says, "Umm, boy that tastes good."

I said, "Yeah, yer right. It's a corker, all right!"

Neither one of us knew how to hold the cigarette in our mouth, so the next thing ya know Pusshead starts yellin' at DJ for getting the cigarette wet. He uses a derogatory term that neither DJ or I had ever heard before. It sounded pretty funny though, so the both of us started laughin'. Well, Pusshead gets mad because he thinks we're laughin' at him instead of the remark he made about the wet cigarette. Next thing ya know Pusshead shoves DJ and me, and that's when Fisty gives Pusshead a quick left hook to the jaw. Well, thankfully it all settled down real fast, and everyone says they're sorry as we continue on towards home. After we walked a couple of hundred feet through the tall brown grass we began to smell something burning. That's when we looked back and saw a grass fire starting. "Holy smokes, the cigarette!" We take off running in the direction of the fire, and now we're all scared as hell. Fear begins to pump our adrenaline as we run towards the rapidly spreading fire.

In the commotion DJ grabs the famous frying pan and uses it to try to beat the flames out. Yep, that's right, the famous "very best fryin' pan!" There we were, full of fear and panic trying to beat out the flames in that tall, dry grass. Next thing you know the wind whips the flames up into the air high above our heads. That's when we started runnin' like hell to save ourselves, and in the process DJ drops the "very best" frying pan. We have to fight with Pusshead to stop him from trying to go back and get it.

"OH MY GOD! OH MY GOD!"

Fisty yells out, "Screw that fryin' pan, the fire's headin' towards the houses. We gotta get help right now!"

My thoughts are in panic, and in my mind I say to myself, *Oh my God! Oh my God!* The others also have looks of fear and panic on their faces. DJ says, "Let's run away and hide someplace!"

Fisty says, "Where the hell to, ya dope? Besides, that's our street where the fire's headin'!"

Well, thank God old Mister Scanlon was retired because he saw the fire and called the fire department right away. We calmed down a little when the fire department began to pull up and started hooking up the big hoses to fight the fire. Putting that fire out took three fire trucks and a bunch of hoses because the wind and dry grass had turned it into a roaring inferno. For at least a half-hour more we were still unsure about what would happen to the houses because it had roared out of control so fast. Those thirty minutes gave us enough time to make another "sacred" pledge to each other. Here we go again!

"Well, no sir, we didn't start that fire. In fact, we almost got burned by it ourselves!"

"Yeah, we had to run fast just to get over here to the street!"

"Just what were you boys doin' over there in the field?"

"Oh, we were just takin' a hike, that's all. You know, just like in the Boy Scouts."

We figured that the mention of an organization as respected as the Boy Scouts would throw him off the trail. Well, that didn't work; we could tell that the fire chief wasn't buyin' the malarkey, but he couldn't prove anything because all of a sudden Mister Scanlon came over and covered for us.

"I'm the one who called the alarm in, Chief. The boys are tellin' the truth; they had to run because the flames jumped up so fast." Wow, were we ever surprised by what Mister Scanlon said to help us out.

After the fire chief left us Mister Scanlon said, "Fisty, Jimmy, how old are you boys?"

Fisty said, "We're both thirteen, Mister Scanlon."

"Oh, I thought you were both older because you're so big for your age. Well, I figured you kids probably started the fire by accident because I saw all of you run back to try and put it out."

Jimmy Finnegan had a quizzical look on his face. "But, Mister Scanlon, what's our age got ta do with it?"

"Jimmy, it seems there just aren't any young men around the neighborhood anymore because of that damned war. I didn't want to see you boys get into any trouble with the law. I figured it might not be long before you kids have to go into the military yourselves since that war just keeps draggin' on. Besides, there wasn't any damage to anyone's house, only the dry grass. So, no harm done, thank God."

"Geez, thanks Mister Scanlon. Yer an all right guy."

"Oh, that's okay, Fisty. By the way how's yer brother Gerry doin' in the Marines these days?"

He's doin' okay. He's in some place called Saipan. At least we think so, but we're not really sure."

He asked about Dad, Joe, Tom and Phil, and I told them they were all safe and doin' okay—so far.

"How's your Uncle Jim holdin' up these days, Jackie?"

I lowered my head as I said, "As well as can be expected, Mister Scanlon." I had heard adults use that expression while talking to a person whose relative was killed in the war. Mister Scanlon had a surprised look on his face because of such a mature answer. He began to confide things that we had never known about.

"Ya know, Jackie, your uncle Jim and I served together in the First World War, but we didn't even know it until the war was over and done with. We even fought in the same division against the Germans at a place called Saint Mihiel in France. That was a real bad place where so many of our friends lost their lives, and now . . ." His voice trailed off, and he had a far-off look in his eyes. "We lost a lot of buddies while we were takin' that damned mountain!" It was as if he was talking to the trees or the sky, because he just kept looking up in the air. I thought I spotted a tear beginning to build up in his eyes—the way it does just before you cry. Suddenly he shook it off, and then he acted as though he was just waking up after a deep sleep.

"Oh, I guess I must be gettin' old. I shouldn't be tellin' you boys about those sad things from the past. The world's got enough trouble goin' on right now."

We all stood around in silence, just staring down at the ground. The four of us boys began to relax a little from the scare we had from that fire. He could sense that we were really affected by what had happened in the field, and only after we had started to walk home did we realize that he had been trying to calm us down.

"Boys, I don't want to sound like a preacher, but please be careful now. And don't get yourselves hurt, there's already enough of that because of the war. And be sure to say hello to everyone for me, will ya, now?"

"Sure, Mister Scanlon. We'll be seein' ya. And thanks fer everything."

"God bless you boys."

Because of old Mister Scanlon we had a lot to think about as we walked home that day. We realized that the loss of so many very young men in the war was on his mind. He was just trying as best he could to protect those of us who would be the next to go. It seemed as if there was always someone like Mister Scanlon around trying to look out for us. Because of that, no matter what happened out there in the rest of the world we always felt safe in our neighborhood.

The fun days of summer rolled on into August, a time of year when changes in the season are noticed most by young boys not wanting September to come. The sun didn't wake us up so early in the morning, and in the afternoon there were longer shadows on the grass. The leaves on the trees began to lose their dark color, and a few even began to drop down into the street. The streetlights came on earlier to cut short our fun games on the street. Reminders about going back to school were everywhere. We just knew that nuns armed with board pointers were waiting for us just around the corner. Those last two weeks of August freedom were the weeks that we tried to savor the most. Since we were now leery about going to the field anymore this summer, we spent more time at Caz Park where we could find pick-up games of football, baseball, and of course our old friend at Caz Creek, "The Old Log." In the evening we'd head over to Uncle Jim's front porch where we'd talk more about the railroad, the First World War, fly fishing and the news about how the war was going. We'd also talk about our fears and worries about our relatives, but now that subject was becoming much more difficult for Uncle Jim to talk about.

-CHAPTER NINETEEN-

GONE, BUT NOT FORGOTTEN

A letter from Dad!

Dear Jackie,

How ya doin', son? Things are going as well as can be expected over here. We think we've got the Germans on the run now, and maybe we'll get this war over real soon! All of us will be so happy when it's over and done with. How's Uncle Jim holdin' up these days, Jackie? I know from the letters from you and Mom that you and the other boys have been staying real close to him, and I'm glad, son. He sent me a letter last week, and it was so sad that it made me want to cry. He talked about when Jimmy was your age and all the fun they had, doing the same things that he's been doing lately with you boys. He's had a real tough life, what with Aunt Margaret dying first, and now his only boy passing away. Please stay real close to him, would you, Jackie?

Son, I just can't tell you how much I miss you and all of the family. I think about all of you every single day, especially in the evening when I'm ready to turn in. I worry about everyone being safe in the house, and under God's protection. You know, I never thought I'd want to see one of those big red busses again, but last night I had a dream that I was driving one down Seneca Street and waving to all of you kids as I passed by. I even saw Mom there with all of you in my dream. You were all smiling and waving back to me, and when I woke up I felt really good for the first time in many months.

Let's hope my dream comes true real soon! God bless and keep you till we all meet again, Son.

All my love,
Dad

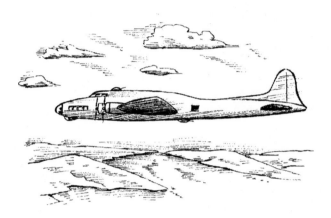

On August twnety-fifth, the day after the letter from Dad, Uncle Jim and I were talking on his front porch when the telegram came to our house from the war department. The two words that have been chiseled into my memory ever since that day are "presumed dead." Mom had not yet gone to work, so she was alone at home when it came. She sent DJ down to bring me home.

"Jackie, your mom wants you to come home right away!" He was out of breath as though he had been running, and right away that made me think the worst.

My heart was beating faster and faster as I said, "What is it? What happened, DJ?"

"I don't know, Jackie. Yer mom said to come home right away!"

Later on he told me that he had lied, and that he had seen the man deliver the telegram and heard my mom crying near the front door. He said he just didn't have the courage to say what it was, even though he was certain what the news was. My worst fears were being played out over and over again as we ran down the street together. When we got to my house he said, "Do you want me to come in with you, Jackie?"

"Yeah, would ya, DJ? Thanks, buddy."

My worst fears were realized as I read those two crushing words that would stay in my mind for the rest of my life. We hugged and cried, and as the rest of the kids came home we hugged and cried again. The first question on all of our minds was what were we going to do now without our dad? We couldn't think straight, and we felt that our whole world had been shattered with the delivery of that little piece of paper. Fisty and Jimmy and Uncle Joe and Aunt Mary and Uncle Jim came to our house, and with each new visitor we started crying all over again. I hadn't yet shown Uncle Jim the letter that I had gotten from Dad, because DJ had come to get me just as I was about to read it to him. He put his arm over my shoulders as he said,

"Jackie, would you read that letter to us now?" He saw that I just wasn't able to read it. "Would you give the letter to me, son? I'll read it." As he read the part about Dad's dream, we all began to cry again.

When he finished reading the letter he held it up in the air as he handed it back to me and said, "Keep these words here in your heart everyone, not that telegram. This is the way we should always remember him."

As had been done for Jimmy there would be just a memorial service. We learned that Dad's plane was on the way back to base from a mission when the mishap occurred. Eyewitness accounts from the other plane's crewmembers reported that Dad's plane had exploded in mid-air for some unknown reason. The formation had just cleared the Normandy coast, heading west over the Channel. It was reported that the explosion happened instantaneously and that there were no parachutes, only debris falling down into the water. The location was approximately one to two miles west of the Normandy coast. In a very low voice Uncle Jim said what we were all thinking.

"Mike and Jimmy, just a few months and a couple of miles apart . . . "

From that day on Uncle Jim and I knew without saying so that we needed each other more than ever now.

Once again Saint Bridget's was full to capacity because of so many friends and relatives: people from the neighborhood, railroad men who knew him, fellow bus drivers, and even people who got to know him just by riding the bus to work. Dad's uncle Joe delivered the eulogy that day, and we were all taken by surprise at his eloquence. We just knew that he had put a lot of thought into the meaning of the war long before Dad had been killed. As he spoke there was complete silence in the church.

"Here's to the heroes in our family—they're both just 'one of the boys.'

"You know, there are times when I wonder just who were those men in the plane that went down near Normandy? What were they like? What were their backgrounds? What did they do for work before this war came upon us? Well, all of us here today know that one of them dear to us was Michael Rossiter: family man, husband, father, and friend. Mike was a bus driver—just an average guy. He was much the same as all the other average guys who have been giving of themselves in this war to help others. Just like young Jimmy McDonald, Mike would have been embarrassed if you had ever referred to him as a hero. But, like Jimmy and his fellow crewmembers on that bomber, heroes are usually just common men from common backgrounds who give uncommon service to their fellow man. Their heroic actions are a testimony to the ultimate expression of what they stand for.

"My nephew, Michael Rossiter, was the youngest son of my brother, Patrick Rossiter, and his wife Margaret. Pat and Margaret passed away when Michael was just a young lad. When he was sixteen years old, Mike was brought to America from an orphanage in Hamilton, Canada. He entered this country illegally, by hiding in the bottom of a hay wagon, and for many years afterwards he worried constantly about not having proper citizenship. He felt so guilty about it. Mike talked to me about this on many occasions, but his first concern was to not cause trouble for the people who had helped him come to this country. Well, then came a time when he heard about an amnesty program, and how you could become a citizen by serving in the military. In spite of being middle-aged and having five children, he volunteered for the Air Corps. He felt that he was indebted to this country for the opportunity given to him, and to his family. He had a sense of obligation because he so appreciated being able to live in this free country of ours. He wanted to earn his citizenship, and that he did.

"It's been over twenty years now since Mike and I made that trip from Hamilton to Buffalo in that old hay wagon. Yes, that's right, I'm the one he worried about getting into trouble because of what we did together that day. And I'll tell you this: I'm glad that I did it, and I'd do it all over again. And for certain I'll say that you, Michael, have made each and everyone of us proud by what you did to earn your deepest wish. You are indeed a man of integrity. All of us here today will miss you so very much. And Michael, in the deepest sense of the word, you are now truly a citizen of this country . . . and you earned it, son."

There were others who spoke during that service, but none so eloquent as Uncle Joe. He caught everyone by surprise, and caused so many tears that day. But, that seemed to be the hallmark of those days of turmoil: So many people would rise to the occasion when needed. Whether it was an average person going off to fight the war, or some other average person doing something to support others at home. That day, as well as many days after was just a blur to me, as I'm sure they were to the rest of the family. Although it wasn't easy, I still believe to this day that what I had been taught by example in that neighborhood enabled me to cope with such a tragic loss.

A few weeks later Mom received a package from Dad's squadron commander containing Dad's personal effects, along with a note from the colonel. The note mentioned Dad's devotion to duty and his fellow crewmembers, as well as his constant talk about his family to the other guys in the group. What was a surprise to us was that the Hamilton pocket watch, which we had bought for him, was among his personal effects. The colonel said that he was told by other crewmembers that Dad would never wear it on a mission because he was afraid of losing it, especially if he were forced to bail out and was captured. The colonel said, "That watch was so very important to him, and after reading the inscription I can see why."

There wasn't any talk about heroism or medals for Dad, but that didn't bother any of us. He was our hero even before he went away to that war, and we didn't need any confirmation of that. Although I was able to cope eventually, the many things with which I had occupied myself as a boy just didn't hold the same interest as they once had now that my dad was gone. I had focused so much on the day when he would return home that the field, the river, "The Old Log" and the park were never the same to me after that. My world of playful boyhood innocence was slowly draining away. I sensed that the same effect was true for my brother and sisters.

-CHAPTER TWENTY-

THE AFTERMATH

After a few weeks I slowly started getting together again with my buddies, but the old fun and games just weren't the same anymore. I began to realize that the beginning of the end of my boyhood had started with the news of Dad's death. I suspected that the beginning of my early entry into adulthood had also begun—and all of this at the age of nine years. Like myself, so many of the young people of those times had to mature all too quickly—before the end of their childhood. Nonetheless, the four of us boys stayed close to each other—and even closer still to Uncle Jim. He had now become a father to at least the three of us. Jimmy's family was one of the few families not affected so terribly by the war, so that he had a reasonably normal childhood. Of course, his cross to bear in life was his awful facial disfigurement. During that time we had stopped using his derogatory nickname. Actually, we had reached a point in time when we were ready to get into a fight with anyone else using it because he had now become our good friend. A fight was seldom necessary though because nobody in all of South Buffalo wanted to tangle with Fisty.

You know, so often in life things just don't work out as we think they will. There are times when we're so certain in our own minds that we have it all figured out, but then . . .

In nineteen forty-five Gerry Mullaney was killed in action at a place called Iwo Jima. That war had such strange irony, at least for our families. You see, Joe Rossiter was finally liberated from a Japanese POW camp on Iwo Jima by that same Marine unit that

Gerry Mullaney had belonged to! Fisty always said that Gerry would someday help Joe.

The twins, Phil and Tom Rossiter, came home from the war in Europe without injury, at least not injury of the physical kind. All of the returning boys had constant nightmares, and would wake up during the night in a cold sweat. Joe, understandably, suffered the worst nightmares. We could only guess what he had gone through during the two years that he had been a prisoner of the Japanese.

I'll never forget that day in nineteen forty-five when we saw him for the first time in over two years. The sight of his emaciated body scared the hell out of me and confirmed my worst nightmares. I actually bawled like a baby when he smiled and gave me a big hug out in front of his house that day. His head drooped down, and his voice was scratchy like an old man's voice as he spoke in a very subdued way. "Hello, Jackie, how ya doin? It's good to see ya. It sure is good to be home again."

His weight had dropped to about seventy pounds, and his bones showed prominently over his five-foot, ten-inch frame. Rifle butts to the mouth had broken his jaw and all of his front teeth at the gum line. Because of that he had suffered from something called Pyorrhea, a severe infection of the gums and tooth sockets. For the rest of my life I never forgot that strange-sounding word because of the connection to Joe's pathetic-looking body. His eyes looked as though they had retreated back into their sockets, and just the simple act of walking brought a look of pain to his scarred face. Aunt Mary later described to my mom the scars all over his body from being constantly whipped. Following the war he lived in daily misery due to all of the many physical problems that he had come home with, especially the parasites that had infected his body. He never did gain back very much of his original one hundred and fifty pounds, and he passed away at the age of fifty-one from the effects of so many medical complications. Not since those days of war have I been in the habit of using derogatory words to describe my fellow man, but to this very day because of the ever-vivid memory of seeing my cousin in that condition, have I ever regretted using those phrases as a young boy. You simply had to live during those times to *really* understand it.

You know, if I had tried to guess just who would be killed or wounded during that war I probably would have guessed one or more of my Rossiter cousins. That they all made it home alive was something of a miracle to all of us. Since all three had become involved so early in the war, and since Joe was often times thought to be already dead, it would have been the logical conclusion. The death of the famous Sullivan boys probably reinforced those thoughts in our minds, but of course none of us actually put those thoughts into words. It was more a case of much of the worry on the part of everyone going to those three boys for such a long period of time. But, far and away, the most shock and disbelief came with the unexpected death of Father Johnny in February of nineteen forty-six.

We had just had our very first (party-line) telephone installed, and one of the first calls to come was at three in the morning on the sixteenth of February. Uncle Joe called to say that Johnny had taken ill suddenly, and had been rushed to the hospital. He died just a few hours later from the kidney failure that had claimed so many from the Rossiter families. He had been a priest for less than two years when God took him from us. All of the families were heartbroken and stricken with grief because it was so shockingly unexpected, and his illness had been in remission. Unexpected tragedy is always the most difficult to accept. Then there was the blessed relief that had come with the end of the war and the assumption that there would be no more death for the young people. For me personally, Johnny's death ranked right up there with the death of my own dad.

This time there would be a Mass for the dead at Saint Bridget's. In fact, it was a Mass like none of us had ever seen before. It was called a Solemn High Requiem Mass, practiced only when burying members of the religious community. The Bishop of the Diocese conducted the service. Mike and I were offered the chance to be involved in the ceremony, but we declined because we were just too heartbroken. We couldn't go through with it because we knew that we would surely break down at some point during the ceremony. The altar was crowded with Johnny's fellow seminarians—his classmates from college who were now young priests as he had been. We knew from the expressions on their faces and the tears in their eyes that they were as shocked and as heartbroken as the rest of us. I couldn't bear to look in the direction of Uncle Joe and Aunt Mary. At times they were crying with their heads bowed down, and at other times their faces were as white as snow while they stared in disbelief towards the altar. They had suffered through such prolonged mental anguish over Joe, and then relief when the boys returned from the war. And now they had to bear this devastating loss of such a fine person. Their world had been on an emotional roller coaster for so long, and now they were losing such a fine young man in a shocking and unexpected instant.

My three buddies and I weren't ashamed when we cried that day. We had all so appreciated the way in which Johnny had treated us as equals, and how he tried to teach and guide us through those years of war that had us in a constant state of fear. After his death, every time we played touch football in the street we thought about and reminisced about our good friend and teacher who had cared so much for us. It would prove impossible for us to forget Johnny and all that he had done for us.

About three months after the death of Father Johnny, a routine follow-up visit at the hospital revealed no trace of my kidney problem. The same disease that had taken Johnny, and that would claim my sister Maureen thirty years later, had gone into remission. I know that Mom said a lot of prayers for me—I don't know. I sometimes wonder though why I was the only one . . .

In the summer of that same year my brother Mike was struck in the side of the face by a carelessly swung bat. The batter had been called out on pitched strikes without swinging. He was disgusted with the call and swung the bat once more in anger just as Mike was moving forward to throw the ball around the bases, as was the practice after a strike out. The blow from the bat cracked

Mike's sinuses in spite of the facemask that he was wearing. Mike developed sinus problems and suffered bad headaches for several years afterwards. I don't know whether he lost his nerve, or was in too much pain to play after that day. The pro scouts who had been coming year after year were not seen very much after that, and soon they weren't seen at all. Whatever the cause, Mike stopped playing ball for good following that incident. By nineteen forty-nine his sinus problem was beginning to abate and he would soon become eligible for the draft, so he decided to follow in Dad's footsteps by enlisting in the Air Force. In a few years he ended up in the middle of the Korean War. He could never tolerate the politician's term "Korean *Conflict*," and neither could I. After all that our people had been through, the politicians were afraid of using the word "war." One thing was certain: We had all had enough of wars by that time.

In the years following the final World War Two victory, the four of us boys stayed close together as buddies, even into the same high school. We had become bonded together because of our shared fears during that terrible war. In nineteen forty-seven, Fisty's dad passed away. The booze had finally taken its toll. His death served to reinforce even more our relationship with Uncle Jim. Three of us were now without a father, so during those years following the war it was as though the three of us had become Uncle Jim's sons.

When the Korean War broke out in nineteen fifty, Fisty and Jimmy enlisted in the Marines together. Corporal James Edward Finnegan and Sergeant John Patrick Mullaney were "killed in action" at some long-forgotten hill or ridge with a strange-sounding name. The wording in the telegrams had not changed since that first one to Uncle Joe and Aunt Mary in nineteen forty-three. Our buddies were only nineteen years old, and now they were gone forever. All of the wonderful memories came flooding back over me—especially that day at the railroad bridge when Fisty thought I had died. Uncle Jim, DJ and I felt the loss of Fisty and Jimmy as though we were brothers and father. DJ and I were juniors in high school; our grief overwhelmed us for months. War continued to claim so many young men. We wondered how long this waste of lives was going to continue?

Following our graduation from high school in nineteen fifty-three, DJ and I went to work on the railroad, in the control towers of course. Uncle Jim had recently retired, but he still had plenty of friends who could help us get the jobs. That's the way the railroad hiring worked in those days. If you knew someone who was presently employed you had the inside track. Of course, the both of us were already "qualified," as the expression went, to work most of the towers by ourselves—thanks to all of those adventurous trips to work at such a young age. We hadn't even given a thought to going to college because it was way beyond our means. Besides, we figured that we were about to earn our fortune!

The pay was more than most average people were earning back then, about three dollars and forty cents per hour. For working holidays we received time-and-one-half pay, and we thought we were on the road to becoming millionaires! Well, anyway, it did help me to buy an old car after several months. When DJ saw my bucket of bolts he asked, "Did the salesman tell you to bring your own rope when you picked it up, Jackie?" But I didn't care what anyone said; you're always proud of your very first car.

The most pride came though when all of us kids were able to help Mom buy the house at number eighty-one that we had rented for so long. We had pooled our money for two years to do it, and when the day finally arrived we couldn't help but recall the Hamilton pocket watch for dad in nineteen forty-three. Mom had finally achieved her dream: A "proper home of our own." When the war came to an end, Mom had to return to her waitress job since there wasn't any need for fighter planes anymore.

The jobs that DJ and I enjoyed so much on the railroad were on shaky ground, and we suspected it all along. Following the war, the trucking industry began taking business away from the railroads, and automation technology was rapidly making the individual control towers obsolete. There had been a long, slow decline going on in the lake freighter business, and the most interesting place, River Bridge Tower, would soon be gone, a victim of the times.

River Bridge was for me a nostalgic place where I had been introduced to railroading—and the famous Jack O'Shea. After all these years the memories of that place are still fresh in my mind. DJ and I knew that it would be only a matter of time, so that when we received our termination notice in nineteen fifty-six, it didn't come as a surprise. We had talked about it on and off, and we didn't want to be drafted into the army. The possibility that you would be drafted was usually enhanced if you were unemployed. Because of what had happened to Jimmy and Fisty and Gerry, we didn't want any part of the army or the Marines. We decided on the Air Force to fulfill our obligation since Dad and Mike had already served there. Mike told us that it would probably be the safest branch to go into. He had been discharged in nineteen fifty-three and was working as a stationary engineer at a local factory. He didn't talk much about sports anymore, and he seemed more quiet and withdrawn—and maybe a little distant. I noticed that he had taken to "stopping in" after work, and that habit would mark the beginning of a long road down for him, but back then I had no idea how far down that road it would eventually be. He had changed since the days before the Korean War. That change in him would continue.

-CHAPTER TWENTY-ONE-

THE END OF AN ERA,

THE BEGINNING OF ANOTHER

When we said our goodbyes that day as we left for basic training in Texas, we couldn't help but think of the many goodbyes of the past. This time it was DJ and I leaving while the others stayed behind, just as we ourselves had done so many times in the past. The role reversals that day made all of us aware of how our lives were changing now. We were not only saying goodbye to Mom and Uncle Jim, Uncle Joe and Aunt Mary, Kitty Corrigan and the others; we were also saying goodbye to a way of life. Only in the future do we realize the deeper meaning of those important times of our lives. And now that understanding gives me insight as to why I can still recall how afraid we were that day as our train pulled away from the station.

After several weeks of basic training we were sent to Alabama for several months of school to learn to be medical technicians. After testing we had been assigned to the medical field, and we were to be known as "Corpsman." What made us really happy was that we were also classified as "non-combatants." We had seen and heard enough about "combat" during our boyhood years to know that it wasn't romantic or exciting—it was only painful and heartbreaking.

We returned home for a ten-day leave in June before we were to depart for our first "permanent party" assignment in eastern France. We were elated when we received our orders before leaving for home, but we didn't tell the family what our destination would be because we wanted to surprise everyone. Shortly after we excitedly told Uncle Jim about our destination, we noticed that he became more quiet and thoughtful. By this time we had become so close to him that DJ and I realized afterwards that the mention of France must have stirred up sad memories for him. We had been so excited, so young, and so inexperienced that we had overlooked such a possibility. But, then we thought of a perfect way to change the mood—"The Old Log!"

We didn't get much fishing done that day because we spent so many hours talking and reminiscing about that first day when Uncle Jim came and caught the huge black bass. We talked about all the good times at the railroad, especially The Bailey Avenue Yards and the River Bridge Tower. We talked about all of the young people that we knew so long ago—or did it just seem like so long ago? We had become so close to Uncle Jim that we confided in him about the fire in the field, and even the death of Joey Sweeney near the railroad bridge. He listened patiently to our explanation about our reasoning that day, and after we finished he thought for a few moments before giving us his advice.

"Boys, ya know you're gonna find that life is not always so well defined, especially when you're young. In time you'll discover that life is constantly full of challenges, choices, temptations and decisions. It's very difficult to say whether you did the right thing or not that day. I'll say this though; that the important thing was that you all discussed it between yourselves before you decided what to do. I can tell from the way you feel now that you're still troubled by your decision. You know, I think it's best to try to put it behind you now because it won't help to be second-guessing yourselves for the rest of your lives. From what you told me it sounds as if that young boy was beyond help before you even found him. It's over and done with now, so like they say, don't cry over spilt milk, just go on from there and keep tryin' ta do what's right in life. We can never be absolutely certain about the decisions that we make. That's 'cause we're all just human. Only God knows the right answer for sure. All we can do is keep tryin' ta do what we think is right, boys."

Suddenly a thought came into my mind about someone who would always be associated in our minds with "The Old Log"— someone we hadn't thought about in several years. "Uncle Jim, have you seen that motorcycle cop, Mickey Dillon, lately?"

"No Jackie, I haven't seen him in a long time now, and I don't know what became of him. I'll have ta remember ta ask around about him. Say, did you boys know that his only son Pat was killed over there in the Pacific?"

DJ and I were shocked by the news and my voice trailed off as I said, "Oh, we didn't know about that, Uncle Jim."

"Yeah, one of those damned Jap Kamikaze planes crashed into his anti-aircraft battery." We all became lost in our own thoughts after he said that. That was the first time we had not known about the death of some young man until several years afterwards. I suppose the reason was because we hadn't visited "The Old Log" in so many years—and probably because Uncle Jim had been so lost himself following the death of Jimmy. I thought about the long delay but decided not to mention it because it would mean dwelling needlessly on another death. There are times in life when some things are best left unsaid.

After another hour or so of sitting there with our thoughts and watching our lines for a bite, Uncle Jim started the conversation up once again. We could tell by the sound of his voice that he had been doing some deep thinking before he spoke.

"Boys, there's somethin' I been wantin' ta tell ya. It's been on my mind for a long time now." He had a real serious look on his face, and his eyebrows were drawing downward.

"What? What's the matter, Uncle Jim?" He paused for several seconds to think about what he wanted to say.

"Well, ya see boys, for a long time now I've been wantin' ta go back ta France for one last visit. You know, I'd really like ta actually see Jimmy's grave—and maybe even the grave of my old buddy, Tommy Ryan, at Saint Mihiel. Years ago the army sent me pictures of Jimmy's grave, but after thinkin' about it I realized that I have to go there. *I need to touch the grave.* Ya know what I mean, boys?" As he asked the question he paused and looked over his shoulder at us. We could see the tears beginning to well up in his eyes, and that in turn caused the same effect on us.

"I been puttin' it off for a long time 'cause I didn't want to go there alone. But, I've been thinkin' ever since you told me about yer assignment that . . . uh, well . . . uh, maybe you boys could go with me? He had been shy about asking us—as though he was testing the water. But, before we could answer the question the tone of his voice changed suddenly, and he became more positive and upbeat.

"Why heck, who knows, maybe I'll just show up there one day and the three of us can go visit them together. Whaddya think, boys?"

"Uncle Jim, we'd be proud to visit the graves with you— anytime. In fact, that's a really good idea, Uncle Jim. You just let us know when yer comin', and we'll be all ready ta go!"

"Okay then, it's a deal, boys."

He seemed to relax after that, as though a load had been lifted from his shoulders. After that we talked about old times, and other small talk. It was a nice sunny day, and we didn't want it to end so we lingered there until the sun began to set. When we got to his house on Sage Avenue we said our goodbyes. We stood there watching after him as he walked towards the front porch where we had all spent so many hours together. When he reached the top step he turned back towards us, and in the most serious voice and expression that we had ever seen, he said, "Jackie, DJ, I want you both to promise me something."

"What is it that you want, Uncle Jim?"

"If for some reason I can't make it back ta France I want you both to promise me that you'll make that visit for me. Will ya do that for me, boys?"

"Sure we would, Uncle Jim. But never mind that, you just let us know when you're comin' and we'll be ready. Now, is that a deal?" He smiled at my use of his long-time expression, and then nodded his head before he faded through the doorway. We left early the next morning for New Jersey to catch our plane to France.

After a grueling twenty-four-hour plane ride on a C119 to

Frankfurt, Germany, with a refueling stop at The Azores Islands, we were at long last in Europe. This was pretty exciting stuff for DJ and me since neither one of us had ever been that far away from home. We were able to catch up on our sleep for twelve hours before boarding a train to eastern France. After arriving at the base we settled down into our new way of life during the next two weeks—until that letter came from Mom. We stared at the words with disbelief. A heart attack had taken Uncle Jim from us. DJ and I were affected by the news in the same way—as sons would react upon hearing about the death of their father. Our friend, our teacher, *our dad* was gone. It was so hard for us to believe that we'd never see him again. That gentle man had taught us most of what we knew about the world. We felt such a terrible sense of loss. After a few days we began to feel a very deep void in our life—a feeling of aloneness in this strange place so far away from Sage Avenue and South Buffalo. We resolved to follow through with Uncle Jim's wish.

-CHAPTER TWENTY-TWO-

LOOKING BACK FROM THE CLIFFS ABOVE

"There's the sign. Turn off here, Jackie."

"Okay, DJ."

We drove up a long narrow road, and as we crested over the top of an incline we saw The American Cemetery at Normandy off in the distance. As we approached the gates we knew right away that this place so far away from home was probably the most defining symbol of our past. We began to think about all of the fine young men whom we had known, and who were now gone forever. We knew instinctively that words couldn't possibly reflect the deep emotions that we were feeling, and so we said nothing as we walked towards the entrance. After picking up the information literature we quietly began the search for Jimmy's grave marker. As we walked slowly towards the grave we became aware of an atmosphere of quiet tranquility and peacefulness about this place. We weren't prepared for the sight of so many grave markers—over nine thousand. We had known about the number of graves beforehand, but the impact of *actually seeing them* was still so hard to comprehend.

When we first spotted the name identifying his resting place it was a shocking blow to us even though we thought that we had prepared ourselves for that moment. That so-familiar name in this place so far away from home stared back at us. We could sense the presence of our Uncle Jim as though he was standing right there beside us, ready with some words of wisdom. Our emotions got the best of us.

James Edward McDonald
Lance Corporal
New York
June 6th 1944

For the first time since Father Johnny's funeral we both began
to feel the tears on our cheeks. This time we didn't have any
concern about showing our emotions openly because there were so
many others all around us who were showing the same emotions.
It's that kind of place. After a time we began to just walk aimlessly
until we came to a place called "Garden of the Missing," and that's
when memories of Dad began to come into my mind. We stopped
at the chapel to say a prayer, and we saw an angel; a dove and a
homeward-bound ship. This meant symbolically that peace had
returned, and that the remaining boys were going home. But going
home was not to be for Dad and Jimmy, and the hundreds of
thousands of other American boys who had given their lives. Many
of them would remain in these places forever. Just at that moment
I recalled a line from a poem that my mom had recited to me so
long ago. She had lost her brother in the First World War, and he
was buried in the well-known Flanders Field Cemetery. The poem's

haunting words about the passing of the previous generation seemed to be so fitting at this place—at this time.

We then wandered slowly about, just looking, and silently reading so many names of so many very young men from so many different places in America. Eventually we came upon an overlook above the place called Omaha Beach where thousands of young American boys had died, including Jimmy. DJ and I silently scanned the beach—wondering what sort of hell had existed here on that day. Eventually, my eyes left the beach and focused a few miles out on the water of The Channel. All that I could think of was, "Dad, we all miss you so much . . . God bless you and keep you forever, Dad."

After a few moments I began to recall what Mom had taught me as a small boy about how the Rossiters had lived in Normandy for so many years before going to Ireland. I couldn't help but think of the irony of Dad losing his life on the very same shores from where his ancestors had started their long journey to America over eight hundred years earlier. Then the expression that Dad had taught to me so long ago came flooding back into my mind: "Jackie, everything in life comes full circle and then returns to the beginning." Dad had returned to the beginning, and now I could feel his presence alongside me on these cliffs above the channel. Uncle Jim had brought me here to be near my dad again.

I was startled out of my daydreaming by DJ's voice. "Come on Jackie, we better get goin' now. Don't forget, we need enough time to stop at Saint Mihiel on the way back to the base."

I pulled out Dad's gold Hamilton pocket watch to check the time. DJ gave me a knowing smile, and said, "What time is it, Jackie?"

"It's time for us to be on our way, DJ."

As we drove away slowly down the access road DJ said suddenly, "Look out, Jackie!" I had to swerve sharply to avoid an oncoming car because I hadn't been paying attention to the road. I was trying to prolong the day by looking back towards the cemetery through the rear-view mirror . . .

EPILOGUE

Jackie was discharged from the Air Force in nineteen fifty-nine. He married a girl of Polish ancestry (that's not a typographical error!) and went into the family business. Today he has his memories, along with a baseball from nineteen forty-four and an old Hamilton pocket watch. DJ stayed in the Air Force and entered the Airman Education and Commissioning Program. He became a fighter pilot and eventually attained the rank of Colonel. The most quiet and unassuming member of our group went on to distinguish himself in Vietnam where he became a highly decorated squadron commander. Colonel Daniel Joseph Corrigan was killed in action in nineteen sixty-nine and is buried at Arlington Cemetery. His mom died soon after her son in nineteen seventy. Uncle Joe and Aunt Mary passed away within a few months of each other in nineteen seventy-two. Their children are all gone now, as are the McDonald children. Jackie's mother, Clara, passed away in nineteen eighty. She and Jackie were always very close, especially after the death of his dad. Jackie's brother and sisters have all passed away, and now Jackie is the only one remaining from those days on Sage Avenue. At times he feels lonely and misses all of them so very much. He still wonders why he was the only one in the family to survive the kidney problem.

What helps to sustain him are his fine memories and the knowledge that the good people of that generation taught all of us, by example, a philosophy of life to live by. Thanks to their example we know first hand the meaning of honor, patriotism, perseverance, dedication, integrity, fellowship and friendship. Sure, life was rigorous, difficult and challenging during those times. In fact, each and every day could prove to be a struggle just to survive.

But, as Uncle Jim would say, "How can you fully appreciate a sunny day unless you've experienced a few rainy days?" Amen!

"That was a really nice story, Grandpa. Do you miss all those people now?"

"I sure do, Jackie . . . I sure do. You know, we humans have strange habits, Jackie."

"Why's that, Grandpa?"

"Because we always place the highest value on those people who aren't with us anymore. When the people and the times that we cared for are gone, it's only then that we realize just how much they had meant to us."

There was a chill in the autumn air as they walked towards the car on the green bridge. The tops of the tall trees were swaying in the wind, while purple and gray clouds raced across the October sky. Winter was on the way. He took one last look at "The Old Log" in the distance and smiled to himself. "Come on, Jackie, let's go home and play some touch football."

THE TREES OF OCTOBER

Parting thoughts from The Long Journey Home

The wind blew the trees of October
The time had slipped by so fast
The old house had beckoned me there
I was drawn by the call of the past

To live it once more was a treat
The old house was so good to see
As the leaves danced around in the street
The memories all danced around me

The people have passed and gone now
The months and the years went so fast
Now the only place I can see them
Is when I remember the past

Then the man that I am said to me
It's over and gone . . . can't you see?
Go back to the present right now, son
It's the place where you have to be

But the boy inside that's a part of me
Knows a place in the past where I'm longing to be
It's fun to go there with family and friends
And to see that old gang . . . DJ, Fisty, Jimmy and me

Did it all seem too perfect? Was that other time and place too much like the mythical "Camelot?" Didn't the people of those times have the same petty differences that we all face from time to time? Yes, they probably did, but when there were problems on a personal level, those problems always took a back seat to the most important problem, the war and all of the heartache that it caused. That generation focused on those more important issues of family, neighbors and country. Relationships mattered the most.

And, of course, I was just a boy.

This story is dedicated to all of those brave people of the nineteen forties who watched over us young people while their own sons and daughters were serving in some far-off part of the world. My deepest thanks to all of you.